Selected Stories by
GUY DE MAUPASSANT

Books in this Series:

Selected Stories by O. Henry
Selected Stories by Anton Chekhov
Selected Stories by Guy de Maupassant
Selected Stories by Mark Twain
Selected Stories by Edgar Allan Poe
Selected Stories by Rudyard Kipling
Selected Stories by Saki
Selected Stories by Oscar Wilde
Selected Stories by Honoré de Balzac
Selected Stories by Charles Dickens
Selected Stories by D.H. Lawrence
Selected Stories by H.G. Wells
Selected Stories by Jack London
Selected Stories by Joseph Conrad
Selected Stories by Leo Tolstoy
Selected Stories by Sir Arthur Conan Doyle

Selected Stories by
GUY DE MAUPASSANT

Published by
Rupa Publications India Pvt. Ltd 2014
7/16, Ansari Road, Daryaganj
New Delhi 110002

Sales Centres:
Allahabad Bengaluru Chennai
Hyderabad Jaipur Kathmandu
Kolkata Mumbai

Selection and Introduction copyright © Terry O'Brien 2014

All rights reserved.
No part of this publication may be reproduced, transmitted,
or stored in a retrieval system, in any form or by any means,
electronic, mechanical, photocopying, recording or otherwise,
without the prior permission of the publisher.

ISBN: 978-81-291-3140-9

First impression 2014

10 9 8 7 6 5 4 3 2 1

Printed at Shree Maitrey Printech Pvt. Ltd., Noida

This book is sold subject to the condition that it shall not,
by way of trade or otherwise, be lent, resold, hired out, or otherwise
circulated, without the publisher's prior consent, in any form of binding or
cover other than that in which it is published.

CONTENTS

Introduction		*vii*
1.	The Necklace	1
2.	Bellflower	11
3.	Coco	17
4.	The Confession	22
5.	A Dead Woman's Secret	28
6.	The Dowry	33
7.	The Hairpin	40
8.	The Hand	47
9.	In the Wood	54
10.	Old Mongilet	60
11.	A Piece of String	67
12.	Timbuctoo	75
13.	Two Little Soldiers	83
14.	The Colonel's Ideas	90
15.	Mother Sauvage	96
16.	Useless Beauty	104

17. The Blind Man	124
18. The Donkey	129
19. The Patron	138
20. The Door	144
21. A Sale	150

INTRODUCTION

Henri René Albert Guy de Maupassant (5 August 1850— 6 July 1893) was a French writer. He was indeed the father of the modern short story and one of the form's finest exponents. Maupassant was a protégé of Flaubert. His stories are characterized by economy of style and efficient, effortless dénouements. He wrote around three hundred short stories, six novels, three travel books, and one volume of verse.

This collection displays his lively diversity, with tales that vary in theme and tone, ranging from tragedy and satire to comedy and farce. He portrays the deceptions, hypocrisies and vanities of society. His tales have been televised and have influenced films, operas and rock music. Maupassant remains a favourite even today.

- A man who always tries to please his wife, a woman who craves more and more, and a catastrophic event that changes their lives forever are the fulcrums of the story 'The Necklace'.
- 'Bellflower' is the seemingly straightforward story of a seamstress and her narrative prowess, which then goes on to detail an interesting incident from her past.
- 'Coco' tells the heart-rending tale of a horse called Coco who falls prey to a young scamp's cruel caprices.
- A startling confession of a sister to her sister on her dying bed shocks and stuns in 'The Confession'.
- A deceased woman's body lies in peace, while her son and

daughter discover an astonishing secret about her, in 'A Dead Woman's Secret'.
- 'The Dowry' is the story of a marriage that begins innocently enough, after the payment of a dowry is made, then unravels to reveal an unexpected twist in the end.
- A hairpin in the centre of a gold frame is the protagonist of the story 'The Hairpin' as a man reminisces about the power that this object still holds over him.
- 'The Hand' is about a crime so inexplicable that it borders on the supernatural.
- A suspected flagrant breach of morality leads the mayor to the woods—only to discover a most refreshing take on love in 'In the Wood'.
- 'Old Mongilet' is quirky take on why one should never get married or venture out of Paris, told through the most humorous of incidents.
- 'A Piece of String' is about the tragic irony of one man being accused of doing something he has not, and what that suspicion eventually does to him.
- 'Timbuctoo' is the fascinating story of a negro prisoner, who is never treated as a prisoner because of his acts of valour. It is a story of incredible individuality in times of war.
- A simple take on complex emotions, 'Two Little Soldiers' examines the age-old ideas of love and friendship and how the two may conflict.
- 'The Colonel's Ideas' is a humorous narration by Colonel Laporte, who believes that Frenchmen, especially French soldiers, can do anything for a pretty women.
- Four Prussian soldiers, after the Prussians have conquered the village, are allotted to old Mother Sauvage to live in her home. The arrangement is kindly and warm on both sides, till news of her own son in battle reaches her—and thus comes about the twist in the tale of 'Mother Sauvage'.

- 'Useless Beauty' is one of Maupassant's most feminist short stories. Here a woman questions her husband's dominance and his need to treat her simply as a means to produce children.
- 'The Blind Man' is the simple yet poignant take of the extent to which society can inflict cruelties upon someone who blind.
- Two scamps who are involved in all kinds of shady dealings and duplicitous tricks to make money, come across a poor donkey which also they manage to exploit to the cruellest of ends in 'The Donkey'.
- 'The Patron' is the humorous tale of a state councillor who, in his eagerness to flaunt his position, writes everyone recommendations and ultimately learns his lesson.
- 'The Door' begins with a categorization of different kinds of husbands, throwing light especially on one rare species who treats everything in a unique and witty manner.
- The sale of a woman by the cubic metre, by one drunken man to another, is the ironic tale of the commodification of marriage, wittily captured in the short story 'A Sale'.

1

THE NECKLACE

She was one of those pretty and charming girls born, as though fate had blundered over her, into a family of artisans. She had no marriage portion, no expectations, no means of getting known, understood, loved, and wedded by a man of wealth and distinction; and she let herself be married off to a little clerk in the Ministry of Education. Her tastes were simple because she had never been able to afford any other, but she was as unhappy as though she had married beneath her; for women have no caste or class, their beauty, grace, and charm serving them for birth or family, their natural delicacy, their instinctive elegance, their nimbleness of wit, are their only mark of rank, and put the slum girl on a level with the highest lady in the land.

She suffered endlessly, feeling herself born for every delicacy and luxury. She suffered from the poorness of her house, from its mean walls, worn chairs, and ugly curtains. All these things, of which other women of her class would not even have been aware, tormented and insulted her. The sight of the little Breton girl who came to do the work in her little house aroused heart-broken regrets and hopeless dreams in her mind. She imagined silent antechambers, heavy with Oriental tapestries, lit by torches in lofty bronze sockets, with two tall footmen in knee-breeches sleeping in large arm-chairs, overcome by the heavy warmth of the stove. She imagined vast saloons hung with antique silks, exquisite pieces of furniture supporting priceless ornaments, and small, charming, perfumed rooms, created just for little parties of intimate friends, men who were famous and sought after, whose homage roused every other woman's envious longings.

When she sat down for dinner at the round table covered with a three-days-old cloth, opposite her husband, who took the cover off the soup-tureen, exclaiming delightedly: 'Aha! Scotch broth! What could be better?' she imagined delicate meals, gleaming silver, tapestries peopling the walls with folk of a past age and strange birds in faery forests; she imagined delicate food served in marvellous dishes, murmured gallantries, listened to with an inscrutable smile as one trifled with the rosy flesh of trout or wings of asparagus chicken.

She had no clothes, no jewels, nothing. And these were the only things she loved; she felt that she was made for them. She had longed so eagerly to charm, to be desired, to be wildly attractive and sought after.

She had a rich friend, an old school friend whom she refused to visit, because she suffered so keenly when she returned home. She would weep whole days, with grief, regret, despair, and misery.

One evening her husband came home with an exultant air, holding a large envelope in his hand.

'Here's something for you,' he said.

Swiftly she tore the paper and drew out a printed card on which were these words:

'The Minister of Education and Madame Ramponneau request the pleasure of the company of Monsieur and Madame Loisel at the Ministry on the evening of Monday, January the 18th.'

Instead of being delighted, as her husband hoped, she flung the invitation petulantly across the table, murmuring: 'What do you want me to do with this?'

'Why, darling, I thought you'd be pleased. You never go out, and this is a great occasion. I had tremendous trouble to get it. Everyone wants one; it's very select, and very few go to the clerks. You'll see all the really big people there.'

She looked at him out of furious eyes, and said impatiently: 'And what do you suppose I am to wear at such an affair?'

He had not thought about it; he stammered: 'Why, the dress you go to the theatre in. It looks very nice, to me...'

He stopped, stupefied and utterly at a loss when he saw that his wife was beginning to cry. Two large tears ran slowly down from the corners of her eyes towards the corners of her mouth.

'What's the matter with you? What's the matter with you?' he faltered.

But with a violent effort she overcame her grief and replied in a calm voice, wiping her wet cheeks:

'Nothing. Only I haven't a dress and so I can't go to this party. Give your invitation to some friend of yours whose wife will be turned out better than I shall.'

He was heart-broken.

'Look here, Mathilde,' he persisted. 'What would be the cost of a suitable dress, which you could use on other occasions as well, something very simple?'

She thought for several seconds, reckoning up prices and also wondering for how large a sum she could ask without bringing upon herself an immediate refusal and an exclamation of horror from the careful-minded clerk.

At last she replied with some hesitation: 'I don't know exactly, but I think I could do it on four hundred francs.'

He grew slightly pale, for this was exactly the amount he had been saving for a gun, intending to get a little shooting next summer on the plain of Nanterre with some friends who went lark-shooting there on Sundays.

Nevertheless he said: 'Very well. I'll give you four hundred francs. But try and get a really nice dress with the money.'

The day of the party drew near, and Madame Loisel seemed sad, uneasy and anxious. Her dress was ready, however. One evening her husband said to her: 'What's the matter with you? You've been very odd for the last three days.'

'I'm utterly miserable at not having any jewels, not a single stone, to wear,' she replied. 'I shall look absolutely no one. I would almost rather not go to the party.'

'Wear flowers,' he said. 'They're very smart at this time of the year. For ten francs you could get two or three gorgeous roses.'

She was not convinced.

'No...there's nothing so humiliating as looking poor in the middle of a lot of rich women.'

'How stupid you are!' exclaimed her husband. 'Go and see Madame Forestier and ask her to lend you some jewels. You know her quite well enough for that.'

She uttered a cry of delight.

'That's true. I never thought of it.'

Next day she went to see her friend and told her her trouble.

Madame Forestier went to her dressing-table, took up a large box, brought it to Madame Loisel, opened it, and said: 'Choose, my dear.'

First she saw some bracelets, then a pearl necklace, then a Venetian cross in gold and gems, of exquisite workmanship. She tried the effect of the jewels before the mirror, hesitating, unable to make up her mind to leave them, to give them up. She kept on asking: 'Haven't you anything else?'

'Yes. Look for yourself. I don't know what you would like best.'

Suddenly she discovered, in a black satin case, a superb diamond necklace; her heart began to beat covetously. Her hands trembled as she lifted it. She fastened it round her neck, upon her high dress, and remained in ecstasy at sight of herself.

Then, with hesitation, she asked in anguish: 'Could you lend me this, just this alone?'

'Yes, of course.'

She flung herself on her friend's breast, embraced her frenziedly, and went away with her treasure. The day of the party arrived. Madame Loisel was a success. She was the prettiest woman present, elegant, graceful, smiling, and quite above herself with happiness. All the men stared at her, inquired her name, and asked to be introduced to her. All the Under-Secretaries of State were eager to waltz with her. The Minister noticed her.

She danced madly, ecstatically, drunk with pleasure, with no thought for anything, in the triumph of her beauty, in the pride of her success, in a cloud of happiness made up of this universal homage and admiration, of the desires she had aroused, of the completeness of a victory so dear to her feminine heart.

She left about four o'clock in the morning. Since midnight her husband had been dozing in a deserted little room, in company with three other men whose wives were having a good time. He threw over her shoulders the garments he had brought for them to go home in, modest everyday clothes, whose poverty clashed with the beauty of the ball-dress. She was conscious of this and was anxious to hurry away, so that she should not be noticed by the other women putting on their costly furs.

Loisel restrained her.

'Wait a little. You'll catch cold in the open. I'm going to fetch a cab.'

But she did not listen to him and rapidly descended the staircase. When they were out in the street they could not find a cab; they began to look for one, shouting at the drivers whom they saw passing in the distance.

They walked down towards the Seine, desperate and shivering. At last they found on the quay one of those old nightprowling carriages which are only to be seen in Paris after dark, as though they were ashamed of their shabbiness in the daylight.

It brought them to their door in the Rue des Martyrs, and sadly they walked up to their own apartment. It was the end, for her. As for him, he was thinking that he must be at the office at ten.

She took off the garments in which she had wrapped her shoulders, so as to see herself in all her glory before the mirror. But suddenly she uttered a cry. The necklace was no longer round her neck!

'What's the matter with you?' asked her husband, already half undressed.

She turned towards him in the utmost distress.

'I...I...I've no longer got Madame Forestier's necklace....'

He started with astonishment.

'What! Impossible!'

They searched in the folds of her dress, in the folds of the coat, in the pockets, everywhere. They could not find it.

'Are you sure that you still had it on when you came away from the ball?' he asked.

'Yes, I touched it in the hall at the Ministry.'

'But if you had lost it in the street, we should have heard it fall.'

'Yes. Probably we should. Did you take the number of the cab?'

'No. You didn't notice it, did you?'

'No.'

They stared at one another, dumbfounded. At last Loisel put on his clothes again.

'I'll go over all the ground we walked,' he said, 'and see if I can't find it.'

And he went out. She remained in her evening clothes, lacking strength to get into bed, huddled on a chair, without volition or power of thought.

Her husband returned about seven. He had found nothing.

He went to the police station, to the newspapers, to offer a reward, to the cab companies, everywhere that a ray of hope impelled him.

She waited all day long, in the same state of bewilderment at this fearful catastrophe.

Loisel came home at night, his face lined and pale; he had discovered nothing.

'You must write to your friend,' he said, 'and tell her that you've broken the clasp of her necklace and are getting it mended. That will give us time to look about us.'

She wrote at his dictation.

By the end of a week they had lost all hope.

Loisel, who had aged five years, declared: 'We must see about replacing the diamonds.'

Next day they took the box which had held the necklace and went to the jewellers whose name was inside. He consulted his books.

'It was not I who sold this necklace, Madame; I must have merely supplied the clasp.'

Then they went from jeweller to jeweller, searching for another necklace like the first, consulting their memories, both ill with remorse and anguish of mind.

In a shop at the Palais-Royal they found a string of diamonds which seemed to them exactly like the one they were looking for. It was worth forty thousand francs. They were allowed to have it for thirty-six thousand.

They begged the jeweller not to sell it for three days. And they arranged matters on the understanding that it would be taken back for thirty-four thousand francs, if the first one were found before the end of February.

Loisel possessed eighteen thousand francs left to him by his father. He intended to borrow the rest.

He did borrow it, getting a thousand from one man, five

hundred from another, five louis here, three louis there. He gave notes of hand, entered into ruinous agreements, did business with usurers and the whole tribe of money-lenders. He mortgaged the whole remaining years of his existence, risked his signature without even knowing if he could honour it, and, appalled at the agonizing face of the future, at the black misery about to fall upon him, at the prospect of every possible physical privation and moral torture, he went to get the new necklace and put down upon the jeweller's counter thirty-six thousand francs.

When Madame Loisel took back the necklace to Madame Forestier, the latter said to her in a chilly voice: 'You ought to have brought it back sooner; I might have needed it.'

She did not, as her friend had feared, open the case. If she had noticed the substitution, what would she have thought? What would she have said? Would she not have taken her for a thief?

Madame Loisel came to know the ghastly life of abject poverty. From the very first she played her part heroically. This fearful debt must be paid off. She would pay it. The servant was dismissed. They changed their flat; they took a garret under the roof.

She came to know the heavy work of the house, the hateful duties of the kitchen. She washed the plates, wearing out her pink nails on the coarse pottery and the bottoms of pans. She washed the dirty linen, the shirts and dish-cloths, and hung them out to dry on a string; every morning she took the dustbin down into the street and carried up the water, stopping on each landing to get her breath. And, clad like a poor woman, she went to the fruiterer, to the grocer, to the butcher, a basket on her arm, haggling, insulted, fighting for every wretched halfpenny of her money.

Every month notes had to be paid off, others renewed, time gained.

Her husband worked in the evenings at putting straight a merchant's accounts, and often at night he did copying at twopence-halfpenny a page.

And this life lasted ten years.

At the end of ten years everything was paid off, everything, the usurer's charges and the accumulation of superimposed interest.

Madame Loisel looked old now. She had become like all the other strong, hard, coarse women of poor households. Her hair was badly done, her skirts were awry, her hands were red. She spoke in a shrill voice, and the water slopped all over the floor when she scrubbed it. But sometimes, when her husband was at the office, she sat down by the window and thought of that evening long ago, of the ball at which she had been so beautiful and so much admired.

What would have happened if she had never lost those jewels. Who knows? Who knows? How strange life is, how fickle! How little is needed to ruin or to save!

One Sunday, as she had gone for a walk along the Champs-Elysees to freshen herself after the labours of the week, she caught sight suddenly of a woman who was taking a child out for a walk. It was Madame Forestier, still young, still beautiful, still attractive.

Madame Loisel was conscious of some emotion. Should she speak to her? Yes, certainly. And now that she had paid, she would tell her all. Why not?

She went up to her.

'Good morning, Jeanne.'

The other did not recognize her, and was surprised at being thus familiarly addressed by a poor woman.

'But...Madame...' she stammered. 'I don't know...you must be making a mistake.'

'No...I am Mathilde Loisel.'

Her friend uttered a cry.

'Oh! My poor Mathilde, how you have changed!'

'Yes, I've had some hard times since I saw you last; and many sorrows...and all on your account.'

'On my account! How was that?'

'You remember the diamond necklace you lent me for the ball at the Ministry?'

'Yes. Well?'

'Well, I lost it.'

'How could you? Why, you brought it back.'

'I brought you another one just like it. And for the last ten years we have been paying for it. You realize it wasn't easy for us; we had no money... Well, it's paid for at last, and I'm glad indeed.'

Madame Forestier had halted.

'You say you bought a diamond necklace to replace mine?'

'Yes. You hadn't noticed it? They were very much alike.'

And she smiled in proud and innocent happiness.

Madame Forestier, deeply moved, took her two hands.

'Oh, my poor Mathilde! But mine was imitation. It was worth at the very most five hundred francs!'

2

BELLFLOWER

How strange are those old recollections which haunt us without our being able to get rid of them! This one is so very old that I cannot understand how it has clung so vividly and tenaciously to my memory. Since then I have seen so many sinister things, either affecting or terrible, that I am astonished at not being able to pass a single day without the face of Mother Bellflower recurring to my mind's eye, just as I knew her formerly long, long ago, when I was ten or twelve years old.

She was an old seamstress who came to my parents' house once a week, every Thursday, to mend the linen. My parents lived in one of those country houses called chateaux, which are merely old houses with pointed roofs, to which are attached three or four adjacent farms.

The village, a large village, almost a small market town, was a few hundred yards off and nestled round the church, a red brick church, which had become black with age.

Well, every Thursday Mother Bellflower came between half-past six and seven in the morning and went immediately into the linen room and began to work. She was a tall, thin, bearded or rather hairy woman, for she had a beard all over her face, a surprising, an unexpected beard, growing in improbable tufts, in curly bunches which looked as if they had been sown by a madman over that great face, the face of a gendarme in petticoats. She had them on her nose, under her nose, round her nose, on her chin, on her cheeks, and her eyebrows, which were extraordinarily thick and long and quite gray, bushy and bristling, looked exactly like a pair of mustaches stuck on there by mistake.

She limped, not like lame people generally do, but like a ship pitching. When she planted her great bony, vibrant body on her sound leg, she seemed to be preparing to mount some enormous wave, and then suddenly she dipped as if to disappear in an abyss and buried herself in the ground. Her walk reminded one of a ship in a storm, and her head, which was always covered with an enormous white cap, whose ribbons fluttered down her back, seemed to traverse the horizon from north to south and from south to north at each limp.

I adored Mother Bellflower. As soon as I was up, I used to go into the linen room, where I found her installed at work with a foot warmer under her feet. As soon as I arrived she made me take the foot warmer and sit upon it, so that I might not catch cold in that large chilly room under the roof.

'That draws the blood from your head,' she would say to me.

She told me stories while mending the linen with her long, crooked, nimble fingers; behind her magnifying spectacles, for age had impaired her sight, her eyes appeared enormous to me, strangely profound, double.

As far as I can remember from the things which she told me and by which my childish heart was moved, she had the large heart of a poor woman. She told me what had happened in the village, how a cow had escaped from the cow house and had been found the next morning in front of Prosper Malet's mill looking at the sails turning, or about a hen's egg which had been found in the church belfry without anyone being able to understand what creature had been there to lay it, or the queer story of Jean Pila's dog who had gone ten leagues to bring back his master's breeches which a tramp had stolen while they were hanging up to dry out of doors after he had been caught in the rain. She told me these simple adventures in such a manner that in my mind they assumed the proportions of never-to-be-forgotten dramas, of grand and mysterious poems; and the ingenious stories invented by the poets, which my mother told me in the evening, had none of the flavor, none of the fullness or of the vigor of the peasant woman's narratives.

Well, one Thursday when I had spent all the morning in listening to Mother Clochette, I wanted to go upstairs to her again during the day after picking hazelnuts with the manservant in the wood behind the farm. I remember it all as clearly as what happened only yesterday.

On opening the door of the linen room, I saw the old seamstress lying on the floor by the side of her chair, her face turned down and her arms stretched out, but still holding her needle in one hand and one of my shirts in the other. One of her legs in a blue stocking, the longer one no doubt, was extended under her chair, and her spectacles glistened by the wall, where they had rolled away from her.

I ran away uttering shrill cries. They all came running, and in a few minutes I was told that Mother Clochette was dead.

I cannot describe the profound, poignant, terrible emotion which stirred my childish heart. I went slowly down into the drawing room and hid myself in a dark corner in the depths of a great old armchair, where I knelt and wept. I remained there for a long time, no doubt, for night came on. Suddenly someone came in with a lamp—without seeing me, however—and I heard my father and mother talking with the medical man, whose voice I recognized.

He had been sent for immediately, and he was explaining the cause of the accident, of which I understood nothing, however. Then he sat down and had a glass of liqueur and a biscuit.

He went on talking, and what he then said will remain engraved on my mind until I die. I think that I can give the exact words which he used.

'Ah!' he said. 'The poor woman! She broke her leg the day of my arrival here. I had not even had time to wash my hands after getting off the diligence before I was sent for in all haste, for it was a bad case, very bad.

'She was seventeen and a pretty girl, very pretty! Would anyone believe it? I have never told her story before; in fact, no one but myself and one other person, who is no longer living in this part of the country, ever knew it. Now that she is dead I may be less discreet.

'A young assistant teacher had just come to live in the village; he was good looking and had the bearing of a soldier. All the girls ran after him, but he was disdainful. Besides that, he was very much afraid of his superior, the schoolmaster, old Grabu, who occasionally got out of bed the wrong foot first.

'Old Grabu had already employed pretty Hortense, who has just died here and who was afterward nicknamed Clochette. The assistant master singled out the pretty young girl who was no doubt flattered at being chosen by this disdainful conqueror; at any rate, she fell in love with him, and he succeeded in persuading her to give him a first meeting in the hayloft behind the school at night after she had done her day's sewing.

'She pretended to go home, but instead of going downstairs when she left the Grabus', she went upstairs and hid among the hay to wait for her lover. He soon joined her, and he was beginning to say pretty things to her, when the door of the hayloft opened and the schoolmaster appeared and asked: "What are you doing up there, Sigisbert?" Feeling sure that he would be caught, the young schoolmaster lost his presence of mind and replied stupidly: "I came up here to rest a little among the bundles of hay, Monsieur Grabu."'

'The loft was very large and absolutely dark. Sigisbert pushed the frightened girl to the farther end and said: "Go, there and hide yourself. I shall lose my situation, so get away and hide yourself."'

'When the schoolmaster heard the whispering he continued: "Why, you are not by yourself."

"Yes, I am, Monsieur Grabu!"

"But you are not, for you are talking."

"I swear I am, Monsieur Grabu."

"I will soon find out," the old man replied and, double-locking the door, he went down to get a light.

Then the young man, who was a coward such as one sometimes meets, lost his head, and he repeated, having grown furious all of a sudden: "Hide yourself, so that he may not find you. You will deprive me of my bread for my whole life; you will ruin my whole career! Do hide yourself!"

'They could hear the key turning in the lock again, and Hortense ran to the window which looked out onto the street, opened it quickly and then in a low and determined voice said: "You will come and pick me up when he is gone," and she jumped out.

'Old Grabu found nobody and went down again in great surprise! A quarter of an hour later Monsieur Sigisbert came to me and related his adventure. The girl had remained at the foot of the wall, unable to get up, as she had fallen from the second story, and I went with him to fetch her. It was raining in torrents, and I brought the unfortunate girl home with me, for the right leg was broken in three places, and the bones had come out through the flesh. She did not complain and merely said with admirable resignation: "I am punished, well punished!"

'I sent for assistance and for the workgirl's friends and told them a made-up story of a runaway carriage which had knocked her down and lamed her outside my door. They believed me, and the gendarmes for a whole month tried in vain to find the author of this accident.

'That is all! Now I say that this woman was a heroine and had the fiber of those who accomplish the grandest deeds in history.

'That was her only love affair, and she died a virgin. She was a martyr, a noble soul, a sublimely devoted woman! And if I did not absolutely admire her I should not have told you this story, which I would never tell anyone during her life; you understand why.'

The doctor ceased; Mamma cried, and Papa said some words which I did not catch; then they left the room, and I remained on my knees in the armchair and sobbed, while I heard a strange noise of heavy footsteps and something knocking against the side of the staircase.

They were carrying away Clochette's body.

3

COCO

Throughout the whole countryside the Lucas farm, was known as 'the Manor.' No one knew why. The peasants doubtless attached to this word, 'Manor,' a meaning of wealth and of splendor, for this farm was undoubtedly the largest, richest and the best managed in the whole neighborhood.

The immense court, surrounded by five rows of magnificent trees, which sheltered the delicate apple trees from the harsh wind of the plain, inclosed in its confines long brick buildings used for storing fodder and grain, beautiful stables built of hard stone and made to accommodate thirty horses, and a red brick residence which looked like a little chateau.

Thanks for the good care taken, the manure heaps were as little offensive as such things can be; the watch-dogs lived in kennels, and countless poultry paraded through the tall grass.

Every day, at noon, fifteen persons, masters, farmhands and the women folks, seated themselves around the long kitchen table where the soup was brought in steaming in a large, blue-flowered bowl.

The beasts—horses, cows, pigs and sheep—were fat, well fed and clean. Maitre Lucas, a tall man who was getting stout, would go round three times a day, overseeing everything and thinking of everything.

A very old white horse, which the mistress wished to keep until its natural death, because she had brought it up and had always used it, and also because it recalled many happy memories, was housed, through sheer kindness of heart, at the end of the stable.

A young scamp about fifteen years old, Isidore Duval by name, and called, for convenience, Zidore, took care of this pensioner, gave him his measure of oats and fodder in winter, and in summer was supposed to change his pasturing place four times a day, so that he might have plenty of fresh grass.

The animal, almost crippled, lifted with difficulty his legs, large at the knees and swollen above the hoofs. His coat, which was no longer curried, looked like white hair, and his long eyelashes gave to his eyes a sad expression.

When Zidore took the animal to pasture, he had to pull on the rope with all his might, because it walked so slowly; and the youth, bent over and out of breath, would swear at it, exasperated at having to care for this old nag.

The farmhands, noticing the young rascal's anger against Coco, were amused and would continually talk of the horse to Zidore, in order to exasperate him. His comrades would make sport with him. In the village he was called Coco-Zidore.

The boy would fume, feeling an unholy desire to revenge himself on the horse. He was a thin, long-legged, dirty child, with thick, coarse, bristly red hair. He seemed only half-witted, and stuttered as though ideas were unable to form in his thick, brute-like mind.

For a long time he had been unable to understand why Coco should be kept, indignant at seeing things wasted on this useless beast. Since the horse could no longer work, it seemed to him unjust that he should be fed; he revolted at the idea of wasting oats, oats which were so expensive, on this paralyzed old plug. And often, in spite of the orders of Maitre Lucas, he would economize on the nag's food, only giving him half measure. Hatred grew in his confused, childlike mind, the hatred of a stingy, mean, fierce, brutal and cowardly peasant.

When summer came he had to move the animal about in the pasture. It was some distance away. The rascal, angrier every morning, would start, with his dragging step, across the wheat fields. The men working in the fields would shout to him, jokingly:

'Hey, Zidore, remember me to Coco.'

He would not answer; but on the way he would break off a switch, and, as soon as he had moved the old horse, he would let it begin grazing; then, treacherously sneaking up behind it, he would slash its legs. The animal would try to escape, to kick, to get away from the blows, and run around in a circle about its rope, as though it had been inclosed in a circus ring. And the boy would slash away furiously, running along behind, his teeth clenched in anger.

Then he would go away slowly, without turning round, while the horse watched him disappear, his ribs sticking out, panting as a result of his unusual exertions. Not until the blue blouse of the young peasant was out of sight would he lower his thin white head to the grass.

As the nights were now warm, Coco was allowed to sleep out of doors, in the field behind the little wood. Zidore alone went to see him. The boy threw stones at him to amuse himself. He would sit down on an embankment about ten feet away and would stay there about half an hour, from time to time throwing a sharp stone at the old horse, which remained standing tied before his enemy, watching him continually and not daring to eat before he was gone.

This one thought persisted in the mind of the young scamp: 'Why feed this horse, which is no longer good for anything?' It seemed to him that this old nag was stealing the food of the others, the goods of man and God, that he was even robbing him,

Zidore, who was working.

Then, little by little, each day, the boy began to shorten the length of rope which allowed the horse to graze.

The hungry animal was growing thinner, and starving. Too feeble to break his bonds, he would stretch his head out toward the tall, green, tempting grass, so near that he could smell, and yet so far that he could not touch it.

But one morning Zidore had an idea: it was, not to move Coco any more. He was tired of walking so far for that old skeleton. He came, however, in order to enjoy his vengeance. The beast watched him anxiously. He did not beat him that day. He walked around him with his hands in his pockets. He even pretended to change his place, but he sank the stake in exactly the same hole, and went away overjoyed with his invention.

The horse, seeing him leave, neighed to call him back; but the rascal began to run, leaving him alone, entirely alone in his field, well tied down and without a blade of grass within reach.

Starving, he tried to reach the grass which he could touch with the end of his nose. He got on his knees, stretching out his neck and his long, drooling lips. All in vain. The old animal spent the whole day in useless, terrible efforts. The sight of all that green food, which stretched out on all sides of him, served to increase the gnawing pangs of hunger.

The scamp did not return that day. He wandered through the woods in search of nests.

The next day he appeared upon the scene again. Coco, exhausted, had lain down. When he saw the boy, he got up, expecting at last to have his place changed.

But the little peasant did not even touch the mallet, which was lying on the ground. He came nearer, looked at the animal, threw at his head a clump of earth which flattened out against the white hair, and he started off again, whistling.

The horse remained standing as long as he could see him;

then, knowing that his attempts to reach the nearby grass would be hopeless, he once more lay down on his side and closed his eyes.

The following day Zidore did not come.

When he did come at last, he found Coco still stretched out; he saw that he was dead.

Then he remained standing, looking at him, pleased with what he had done, surprised that it should already be all over. He touched him with his foot, lifted one of his legs and then let it drop, sat on him and remained there, his eyes fixed on the grass, thinking of nothing. He returned to the farm, but did not mention the accident, because he wished to wander about at the hours when he used to change the horse's pasture. He went to see him the next day. At his approach some crows flew away. Countless flies were walking over the body and were buzzing around it. When he returned home, he announced the event. The animal was so old that nobody was surprised. The master said to two of the men: 'Take your shovels and dig a hole right where he is.'

The men buried the horse at the place where he had died of hunger. And the grass grew thick, green and vigorous, fed by the poor body.

4

THE CONFESSION

Marguerite de Thérelles was dying. Although but fifty-six, she seemed like seventy-five at least. She panted, paler than the sheets, shaken by dreadful shiverings, her face convulsed, her eyes haggard, as if she had seen some horrible thing.

Her eldest sister, Suzanne, six years older, sobbed on her knees beside the bed. A little table drawn close to the couch of the dying woman, and covered with a napkin, bore two lighted candles, the priest being momentarily expected to give extreme unction and the communion, which should be the last.

The apartment had that sinister aspect, that air of hopeless farewells, which belongs to the chambers of the dying. Medicine bottles stood about on the furniture, linen lay in the corners, pushed aside by foot or broom. The disordered chairs themselves seemed affrighted, as if they had run, in all the senses of the word. Death, the formidable, was there, hidden, waiting.

The story of the two sisters was very touching. It was quoted far and wide; it had made many eyes weep.

Suzanne, the elder, had once been madly in love with a young man, who had also been in love with her. They were engaged, and were only waiting the day fixed for the contract, when Henry de Lampierre suddenly died.

The despair of the young girl was dreadful, and she vowed that she would never marry. She kept her word. She put on widow's weeds, which she never took off.

Then her sister, her little sister Marguérite, who was only twelve years old, came one morning to throw herself into the arms of the elder, and said: 'Big Sister, I do not want thee to be unhappy. I do not want thee to cry all thy life. I will never leave thee, never, never! I—I, too, shall never marry. I shall stay with thee always, always, always!'

Suzanne, touched by the devotion of the child, kissed her, but did not believe.

Yet the little one, also, kept her word, and despite the entreaties of her parents, despite the supplications of the elder, she never married. She was pretty, very pretty; she refused many a young man who seemed to love her truly; and she never left her sister.

They lived together all the days of their life, without ever being separated a single time. They went side by side, inseparably united. But Marguérite seemed always sad, oppressed, more melancholy than the elder, as though perhaps her sublime sacrifice had broken her spirit. She aged more quickly, had white hair from the age of thirty, and often suffering, seemed afflicted by some secret, gnawing trouble.

Now she was to be the first to die.

Since yesterday she was no longer able to speak. She had only said, at the first glimmers of day-dawn: 'Go fetch Monsieur le Curé, the moment has come.'

And she had remained since then upon her back, shaken with spasms, her lips agitated as though dreadful words were mounting from her heart without power of issue, her look mad with fear, terrible to see.

Her sister, torn by sorrow, wept wildly, her forehead resting on the edge of the bed, and kept repeating: 'Margot, my poor Margot, my little one!'

She had always called her, 'Little One,' just as the younger had always called her 'Big Sister.'

Steps were heard on the stairs. The door opened. A choir boy appeared, followed by an old priest in a surplice. As soon as she perceived him, the dying woman, with one shudder, sat up, opened her lips, stammered two or three words, and began to scratch the sheets with her nails as if she had wished to make a hole.

The Abbé Simon approached, took her hand, kissed her brow, and with a soft voice: 'God pardon thee, my child; have courage, the moment is now come, speak.'

Then Marguérite, shivering from head to foot, shaking her whole couch with nervous movements, stammered: 'Sit down, Big Sister...listen.'

The priest bent down toward Suzanne, who was still flung upon the bed's foot. He raised her, placed her in an armchair, and taking a hand of each of the sisters in one of his own, he pronounced:

'Lord, my God! Endue them with strength, cast Thy mercy upon them.'

And Marguérite began to speak. The words issued from her throat one by one, raucous, with sharp pauses, as though very feeble.

'Pardon, pardon, Big Sister; oh, forgive! If thou knewest how I have had fear of this moment all my life....'

Suzanne stammered through her tears: 'Forgive thee what, Little One? Thou hast given all to me, sacrificed everything; thou art an angel....'

But Marguérite interrupted her: 'Hush, hush! Let me speak...do not stop me. It is dreadful...let me tell all...to the very end, without flinching. Listen. Thou rememberest...thou rememberest...Henry...'

Suzanne trembled and looked at her sister. The younger continued: 'Thou must hear all, to understand. I was twelve years old, only twelve years old; thou rememberest well, is it not so?

And I was spoiled, I did everything that I liked! Thou rememberest, surely, how they spoiled me? Listen. The first time that he came he had varnished boots. He got down from his horse at the great steps, and he begged pardon for his costume, but he came to bring some news to papa. Thou rememberest, is it not so? Don't speak—listen. When I saw him I was completely carried away, I found him so very beautiful; and I remained standing in a corner of the salon all the time that he was talking. Children are strange...and terrible. Oh yes...I have dreamed of all that.

'He came back again...several times...I looked at him with all my eyes, with all my soul...I was large of my age...and very much more knowing than anyone thought. He came back often...I thought only of him. I said, very low: "Henry...Henry de Lampierre!"

'Then they said that he was going to marry thee. It was a sorrow; oh, Big Sister, a sorrow...a sorrow! I cried for three nights without sleeping. He came back every day, in the afternoon, after his lunch...thou rememberest, is it not so? Say nothing...listen. Thou madest him cakes which he liked...with meal, with butter and milk. Oh, I know well how. I could make them yet if it were needed. He ate them at one mouthful, and...and then he drank a glass of wine, and then he said, "It is delicious." Thou rememberest how he would say that?

'I was jealous, jealous! The moment of thy marriage approached. There were only two weeks more. I became crazy. I said to myself: "He shall not marry Suzanne, no, I will not have it! It is I whom he will marry when I am grown up. I shall never find anyone whom I love so much." But one night, ten days before the contract, thou tookest a walk with him in front of the chateau by moonlight...and there...under the fir, under the great fir...he kissed thee...kissed...holding thee in his two arms...so long. Thou rememberest, is it not so? It was probably the first time...yes... Thou wast so pale when thou earnest back to the salon.

'I had seen you two; I was there, in the shrubbery. I was angry! If I could I should have killed you both!

'I said to myself: "He shall not marry Suzanne, never! He shall marry no one. I should be too unhappy." And all of a sudden I began to hate him dreadfully.

'Then, dost thou know what I did? Listen. I had seen the gardener making little balls to kill strange dogs. He pounded up a bottle with a stone and put the powdered glass in a little ball of meat.

'I took a little medicine bottle that mamma had; I broke it small with a hammer, and I hid the glass in my pocket. It was a shining powder...The next day, as soon as you had made the little cakes...I split them with a knife and I put in the glass...He ate three of them...I too, I ate one...I threw the other six into the pond. The two swans died three days after... Dost thou remember? Oh, say nothing...listen, listen. I, I alone did not die...but I have always been sick. Listen... He died—thou knowest well...listen...that, that is nothing. It is afterwards, later...always...the worst...listen.

'My life, all my life...what torture! I said to myself: "I will never leave my sister. And at the hour of death I will tell her all..." There! And ever since, I have always thought of that moment when I should tell thee all. Now it is come. It is terrible. Oh...Big Sister!

'I have always thought, morning and evening, by night and by day, "Some time I must tell her that..." I waited...What agony!... It is done. Say nothing. Now I am afraid...am afraid...oh, I am afraid. If I am going to see him again, soon, when I am dead. See him again...think of it! The first! Before thou! I shall not dare. I must...I am going to die...I want you to forgive me. I want it...I cannot go off to meet him without that. Oh, tell her to forgive me, Monsieur le Curé, tell her...I implore you to do it. I cannot die without that....'

She was silent, and remained panting, always scratching the sheet with her withered nails.

Suzanne had hidden her face in her hands, and did not move. She was thinking of him whom she might have loved so long! What a good life they should have lived together! She saw him once again in that vanished bygone time, in that old past which was put out forever. The beloved dead—how they tear your hearts! Oh, that kiss, his only kiss! She had hidden it in her soul. And after it nothing, nothing more her whole life long!

All of a sudden the priest stood straight, and, with a strong vibrant voice, he cried: 'Mademoiselle Suzanne, your sister is dying!'

Then Suzanne, opening her hands, showed her face soaked with tears, and throwing herself upon her sister, she kissed her with all her might, stammering: 'I forgive thee, I forgive thee, Little One.'

5

A DEAD WOMAN'S SECRET

The woman had died without pain, quietly, as a woman should whose life had been blameless. Now she was resting in her bed, lying on her back, her eyes closed, her features calm, her long white hair carefully arranged as though she had done it up ten minutes before dying. The whole pale countenance of the dead woman was so collected, so calm, so resigned that one could feel what a sweet soul had lived in that body, what a quiet existence this old soul had led, how easy and pure the death of this parent had been.

Kneeling beside the bed, her son, a magistrate with inflexible principles, and her daughter, Marguerite, known as Sister Eulalie, were weeping as though their hearts would break. She had, from childhood up, armed them with a strict moral code, teaching them religion, without weakness, and duty, without compromise. He, the man, had become a judge and handled the law as a weapon with which he smote the weak ones without pity. She, the girl, influenced by the virtue which had bathed her in this austere family, had become the bride of the Church through her loathing for man.

They had hardly known their father, knowing only that he had made their mother most unhappy, without being told any other details.

The nun was wildly kissing the dead woman's hand, an ivory hand as white as the large crucifix lying across the bed. On the other side of the long body, the other hand seemed still to be holding the sheet in the death grasp; and the sheet had preserved the little creases as a memory of those last movements which precede eternal immobility.

A few light taps on the door caused the two sobbing heads to look up, and the priest, who had just come from dinner, returned. He was red and out of breath from his interrupted digestion, for he had made himself a strong mixture of coffee and brandy in order to combat the fatigue of the last few nights and of the wake which was beginning.

He looked sad, with that assumed sadness of the priest for whom death is a bread winner. He crossed himself and approaching with his professional gesture: 'Well, my poor children! I have come to help you pass these last sad hours.' But Sister Eulalie suddenly arose. 'Thank you, 'father, but my brother and I prefer to remain alone with her. This is our last chance to see her, and we wish to be together, all three of us, as we—we—used to be when we were small and our poor mo-mother—'

Grief and tears stopped her; she could not continue.

Once more serene, the priest bowed, thinking of his bed. 'As you wish, my children.' He kneeled, crossed himself, prayed, arose and went out quietly, murmuring: 'She was a saint!'

They remained alone, the dead woman and her children. The ticking of the clock, hidden in the shadow, could be heard distinctly, and through the open window drifted in the sweet smell of hay and of woods, together with the soft moonlight. No other noise could be heard over the land except the occasional croaking of the frog or the chirping of some belated insect. An infinite peace, a divine melancholy, a silent serenity surrounded this dead woman, seemed to be breathed out from her and to appease nature itself.

Then the judge, still kneeling, his head buried in the bed

clothes, cried in a voice altered by grief and deadened by the sheets and blankets: 'Mamma, mamma, mamma!' And his sister, frantically striking her forehead against the woodwork, convulsed, twitching and trembling as in an epileptic fit, moaned: 'Jesus, Jesus, mamma, Jesus!' And both of them, shaken by a storm of grief, gasped and choked.

The crisis slowly calmed down and they began to weep quietly, just as on the sea when a calm follows a squall.

A rather long time passed and they arose and looked at their dead mother. And the memories, those distant memories, yesterday so dear, today so torturing, came to their minds with all the little forgotten details, those little intimate familiar details which bring back to life the one who has left. They recalled to each other circumstances, words, smiles, intonations of the mother who was no longer to speak to them. They saw her again happy and calm. They remembered things which she had said, and a little motion of the hand, like beating time, which she often used when emphasizing something important.

And they loved her as they never had loved her before. They measured the depth of their grief, and thus they discovered how lonely they would find themselves.

It was their prop, their guide, their whole youth, all the best part of their lives which was disappearing. It was their bond with life, their mother, their mamma, the connecting link with their forefathers which they would thenceforth miss. They now became solitary, lonely beings; they could no longer look back.

The nun said to her brother: 'You remember how mamma used always to read her old letters; they are all there in that drawer. Let us, in turn, read them; let us live her whole life through tonight beside her! It would be like a road to the cross, like making the acquaintance of her mother, of our grandparents, whom we never knew, but whose letters are there and of whom she so often spoke, do you remember?'

Out of the drawer they took about ten little packages of yellow paper, tied with care and arranged one beside the other. They threw these relics on the bed and chose one of them on which the word 'Father' was written. They opened and read it.

It was one of those old-fashioned letters which one finds in old family desk drawers, those epistles which smell of another century. The first one started: 'My dear,' another one: 'My beautiful little girl,' others: 'My dear child,' or: 'My dear daughter.' And suddenly the nun began to read aloud, to read over to the dead woman her whole history, all her tender memories. The judge, resting his elbow on the bed, was listening with his eyes fastened on his mother. The motionless body seemed happy.

Sister Eulalie, interrupting herself, said suddenly:

'These ought to be put in the grave with her; they ought to be used as a shroud and she ought to be buried in it.' She took another package, on which no name was written. She began to read in a firm voice: 'My adored one, I love you wildly. Since yesterday I have been suffering the tortures of the damned, haunted by our memory. I feel your lips against mine, your eyes in mine, your breast against mine. I love you, I love you! You have driven me mad. My arms open, I gasp, moved by a wild desire to hold you again. My whole soul and body cries out for you, wants you. I have kept in my mouth the taste of your kisses—'

The judge had straightened himself up. The nun stopped reading. He snatched the letter from her and looked for the signature. There was none, but only under the words, 'The man who adores you,' the name 'Henry.' Their father's name was Rene. Therefore this was not from him. The son then quickly rummaged through the package of letters, took one out and read: 'I can no longer live without your caresses.' Standing erect, severe as when sitting on the bench, he looked unmoved at the dead woman. The nun, straight as a statue, tears trembling in the corners of her eyes, was watching her brother, waiting. Then he crossed the room slowly, went to the window and stood there, gazing out into the dark night.

When he turned around again Sister Eulalie, her eyes dry now, was still standing near the bed, her head bent down.

He stepped forward, quickly picked up the letters and threw them pell-mell back into the drawer. Then he closed the curtains of the bed.

When daylight made the candles on the table turn pale, the son slowly left his armchair, and without looking again at the mother upon whom he had passed sentence, severing the tie that united her to son and daughter, he said slowly: 'Let us now retire, sister.'

6

THE DOWRY

The marriage of Maitre Simon Lebrument with Mademoiselle Jeanne Cordier was a surprise to no one. Maitre Lebrument had bought out the practice of Maitre Papillon; naturally, he had to have money to pay for it; and Mademoiselle Jeanne Cordier had three hundred thousand francs clear in currency, and in bonds payable to bearer.

Maitre Lebrument was a handsome man. He was stylish, although in a provincial way; but, nevertheless, he was stylish—a rare thing at Boutigny-le-Rebours.

Mademoiselle Cordier was graceful and fresh-looking, although a trifle awkward; nevertheless, she was a handsome girl, and one to be desired.

The marriage ceremony turned all Boutigny topsy-turvy. Everybody admired the young couple, who quickly returned home to domestic felicity, having decided simply to take a short trip to Paris, after a few days of retirement.

This tete-a-tete was delightful, Maitre Lebrument having shown just the proper amount of delicacy. He had taken as his motto: 'Everything comes to him who waits.' He knew how to be at the same time patient and energetic. His success was rapid and complete.

After four days, Madame Lebrument adored her husband. She

could not get along without him. She would sit on his knees, and taking him by the ears she would say: 'Open your mouth and shut your eyes.' He would open his mouth wide and partly close his eyes, and he would try to nip her fingers as she slipped some dainty between his teeth. Then she would give him a kiss, sweet and long, which would make chills run up and down his spine. And then, in his turn, he would not have enough caresses to please his wife from morning to night and from night to morning.

When the first week was over, he said to his young companion:

'If you wish, we will leave for Paris next Tuesday. We will be like two lovers, we will go to the restaurants, the theatres, the concert halls, everywhere, everywhere!'

She was ready to dance for joy.

'Oh! Yes, yes. Let us go as soon as possible.'

He continued: 'And then, as we must forget nothing, ask your father to have your dowry ready; I shall pay Maitre Papillon on this trip.'

She answered: 'All right: I will tell him tomorrow morning.'

And he took her in his arms once more, to renew those sweet games of love which she had so enjoyed for the past week.

The following Tuesday, father-in-law and mother-in-law went to the station with their daughter and their son-in-law who were leaving for the capital.

The father-in-law said: 'I tell you it is very imprudent to carry so much money about in a pocketbook.' And the young lawyer smiled.

'Don't worry; I am accustomed to such things. You understand that, in my profession, I sometimes have as much as a million about me. In this manner, at least we avoid a great amount of red tape and delay. You needn't worry.'

The conductor was crying: 'All aboard for Paris!'

They scrambled into a car, where two old ladies were already seated.

Lebrument whispered into his wife's ear: 'What a bother! I won't be able to smoke.'

She answered in a low voice, 'It annoys me too, but not on account of your cigar.'

The whistle blew and the train started. The trip lasted about an hour, during which time they did not say very much to each other, as the two old ladies did not go to sleep.

As soon as they were in front of the Saint-Lazare Station, Maitre Lebrument said to his wife: 'Dearie, let us first go over to the Boulevard and get something to eat; then we can quietly return and get our trunk and bring it to the hotel.'

She immediately assented.

'Oh! Yes. Let's eat at the restaurant. Is it far?'

He answered: 'Yes, it's quite a distance, but we will take the omnibus.'

She was surprised: 'Why don't we take a cab?'

He began to scold her smilingly: 'Is that the way you save money? A cab for a five minutes' ride at six cents a minute! You would deprive yourself of nothing.'

'That's so,' she said, a little embarrassed.

A big omnibus was passing by, drawn by three big horses, which were trotting along. Lebrument called out: 'Conductor! Conductor!'

The heavy carriage stopped. And the young lawyer, pushing his wife, said to her quickly: 'Go inside; I'm going up on top, so that I may smoke at least one cigarette before lunch.'

She had no time to answer. The conductor, who had seized her by the arm to help her up the step, pushed her inside, and she fell into a seat, bewildered, looking through the back window at the feet of her husband as he climbed up to the top of the vehicle.

And she sat there motionless, between a fat man who smelled of cheap tobacco and an old woman who smelled of garlic.

All the other passengers were lined up in silence—a grocer's boy, a young girl, a soldier, a gentleman with gold-rimmed spectacles and a big silk hat, two ladies with a self-satisfied and crabbed look, which seemed to say: 'We are riding in this thing, but we don't have to,' two sisters of charity and an undertaker. They looked like a collection of caricatures.

The jolting of the wagon made them wag their heads and the shaking of the wheels seemed to stupefy them—they all looked as though they were asleep.

The young woman remained motionless.

'Why didn't he come inside with me?' she was saying to herself. An unaccountable sadness seemed to be hanging over her. He really need not have acted so.

The sisters motioned to the conductor to stop, and they got off one after the other, leaving in their wake the pungent smell of camphor. The bus started up and soon stopped again. And in got a cook, red-faced and out of breath. She sat down and placed her basket of provisions on her knees. A strong odor of dish-water filled the vehicle.

'It's further than I imagined,' thought Jeanne.

The undertaker went out, and was replaced by a coachman who seemed to bring the atmosphere of the stable with him. The young girl had as a successor a messenger, the odor of whose feet showed that he was continually walking.

The lawyer's wife began to feel ill at ease, nauseated, ready to cry without knowing why.

Other persons left and others entered. The stage went on through interminable streets, stopping at stations and starting again.

'How far it is!' thought Jeanne. 'I hope he hasn't gone to sleep! He has been so tired the last few days.'

Little by little, all the passengers left. She was left alone, all alone. The conductor cried: 'Vaugirard!'

Seeing that she did not move, he repeated: 'Vaugirard!'

She looked at him, understanding that he was speaking to her, as there was no one else there. For the third time the man said: 'Vaugirard!'

Then she asked: 'Where are we?'

He answered gruffly: 'We're at Vaugirard, of course! I have been yelling it for the last half hour!'

'Is it far from the Boulevard?' she said.

'Which boulevard?'

'The Boulevard des Italiens.'

'We passed that a long time ago!'

'Would you mind telling my husband?'

'Your husband! Where is he?'

'On the top of the bus.'

'On the top! There hasn't been anybody there for a long time.'

She started, terrified.

'What? That's impossible! He got on with me. Look well! He must be there.'

The conductor was becoming uncivil: 'Come on, little one, you've talked enough! You can find ten men for every one that you lose. Now run along. You'll find another one somewhere.'

Tears were coming to her eyes. She insisted: 'But, monsieur, you are mistaken; I assure you that you must be mistaken. He had a big portfolio under his arm.'

The man began to laugh: 'A big portfolio! Oh, yes! He got off at the Madeleine. He got rid of you, all right! Ha! ha! ha!'

The stage had stopped. She got out and, in spite of herself, she looked up instinctively to the roof of the bus. It was absolutely deserted.

Then she began to cry, and, without thinking that anybody was listening or watching her, she said out loud: 'What is going to become of me?'

An inspector approached: 'What's the matter?'

The conductor answered, in a bantering tone of voice:

'It's a lady who got left by her husband during the trip.'

The other continued: 'Oh! that's nothing. You go about your business.'

Then he turned on his heels and walked away.

She began to walk straight ahead, too bewildered, too crazed even to understand what had happened to her. Where was she to go? What could she do? What could have happened to him? How could he have made such a mistake? How could he have been so forgetful?

She had two francs in her pocket. To whom could she go? Suddenly she remembered her cousin Barral, one of the assistants in the offices of the Ministry of the Navy.

She had just enough to pay for a cab. She drove to his house. He met her just as he was leaving for his office. He was carrying a large portfolio under his arm, just like Lebrument.

She jumped out of the carriage.

'Henry!' she cried.

He stopped, astonished: 'Jeanne! Here—all alone! What are you doing? Where have you come from?'

Her eyes full of tears, she stammered: 'My husband has just got lost!'

'Lost! Where?'

'On an omnibus.'

'On an omnibus?'

Weeping, she told him her whole adventure.

He listened, thought, and then asked: 'Was his mind clear this morning?'

'Yes.'

'Good. Did he have much money with him?'

'Yes, he was carrying my dowry.'

'Your dowry! The whole of it?'

'The whole of it—in order to pay for the practice which he bought.'

'Well, my dear cousin, by this time your husband must be well on his way to Belgium.'

She could not understand. She kept repeating: 'My husband—you say—'

'I say that he has disappeared with your—your capital—that's all!'

She stood there, a prey to conflicting emotions, sobbing.

'Then he is—he is—he is a villain!'

And, faint from excitement, she leaned her head on her cousin's shoulder and wept.

As people were stopping to look at them, he pushed her gently into the vestibule of his house, and, supporting her with his arm around her waist, he led her up the stairs, and as his astonished servant opened the door, he ordered: 'Sophie, run to the restaurant and get a luncheon for two. I am not going to the office today.'

7

THE HAIRPIN

I will not record the name either of the country or of the man concerned. It was far, very far from this part of the world, on a fertile and scorching sea-coast. All morning we had been following a coast clothed with crops and a blue sea clothed in sunlight. Flowers thrust up their heads quite close to the waves, rippling waves, so gentle, drowsing. It was hot—a relaxing heat, redolent of the rich soil, damp and fruitful: one almost heard the rising of the sap.

I had been told that, in the evening, I could obtain hospitality in the house of a Frenchman, who lived at the end of a headland, in an orange grove. Who was he? I did not yet know. He had arrived one morning, ten years ago; he had bought a piece of ground, planted vines, sown seed; he had worked, this man, passionately, furiously. Then, month by month, year by year, increasing his demesne, continually fertilizing the lusty and virgin soil, he had in this way amassed a fortune by his unsparing labour.

Yet he went on working, all the time, people said. Up at dawn, going over his fields until night, always on the watch, he seemed to be goaded by a fixed idea, tortured by an insatiable lust for money, which nothing lulls to sleep, and nothing can appease.

Now, he seemed to be very rich.

The sun was just setting when I reached his dwelling. This

was, indeed, built at the end of an out-thrust cliff, in the midst of orange-trees. It was a large plain-looking house, built four-square, and overlooking the sea.

As I approached, a man with a big beard appeared in the doorway. Greeting him, I asked him to give me shelter for the night. He held out his hand to me, smiling.

'Come in, sir, and make yourself at home.'

He led the way to a room, put a servant at my disposal, with the perfect assurance and easy good manners of a man of the world; then he left me, saying: 'We will dine as soon as you are quite ready to come down.'

We did indeed dine alone, on a terrace facing the sea. At the beginning of the meal, I spoke to him of this country, so rich, so far from the world, so little known. He smiled, answering indifferently.

'Yes, it is a beautiful country. But no country is attractive that lies so far from the country of one's heart.'

'You regret France?'

'I regret Paris.'

'Why not go back to it?'

'Oh, I shall go back to it.'

Then, quite naturally, we began to talk of French society, of the boulevards, and people, and things of Paris. He questioned me after the manner of a man who knew all about it, mentioning names, all the names familiar on the Vaudeville promenade.

'Who goes to Tortoni's now?'

'All the same people, except those who have died.'

I looked at him closely, haunted by a vague memory. Assuredly, I had seen this face somewhere. But where? But when? He seemed weary though active, melancholy though determined. His big fair beard fell to his chest, and now and then he took hold of it below the chin and, holding it in his closed hand, let the whole length of it run through his fingers. A little bald, he had heavy eyebrows and a thick moustache that merged into the hair covering his cheeks. Behind us the sun sank in the sea, flinging over the coast a fiery haze. The orange-trees in full blossom filled the air with their sweet, heady scent. He had eyes for nothing but me, and with his intent gaze he seemed to peer through my eyes, to see in the depths of my thoughts, the far-off, familiar, and well-loved vision of the wide, shady pavement that runs from the Madeleine to the Rue Drouot.

'Do you know Boutrelle?'

'Yes, well.'

'Is he much changed?'

'Yes, he has gone quite white.'

'And La Ridamie?'

'Always the same.'

'And the women? Tell me about the woman. Let me see, Do you know Suzanne Verner?'

'Yes, very stout. Done for.'

'Ah! And Sophie Astier?'

'Dead.'

'Poor girl! And is…do you know…'

But he was abruptly silent. Then in a changed voice, his face grown suddenly pale, he went on:

'No, it would be better for me not to speak of it any more, it tortures me.'

Then, as if to change the trend of his thoughts, he rose.

'Shall we go in?'

'I am quite ready.'

And he preceded me into the house.

The rooms on the ground floor were enormous, bare, gloomy, apparently deserted. Napkins and glasses were scattered about the tables, left there by the swan-skinned servants who prowled about this vast dwelling all the time. Two guns were hanging from two nails on the wall, and in the corners I saw spades, fishing-lines, dried palm leaves, objects of all kinds, deposited there by people who happened to come into the house, and remaining there within easy reach until someone happened to go out or until they were wanted for a job of work.

My host smiled.

'It is the dwelling, or rather the hovel; of an exile,' said he, 'but my room is rather more decent. Let's go there.'

My first thought, when I entered the room, was that I was penetrating into a second-hand dealer's, so full of things was it, all the incongruous, strange, and varied things that one feels must be mementoes. On the walls, two excellent pictures by well-known artists, hangings, weapons, swords and pistols, and then, right in the middle of the most prominent panel, a square of white satin in a gold frame.

Surprised, I went closer to look at it and I saw a hairpin stuck in the centre of the gleaming material.

My host laid his hand on my shoulder.

'There,' he said, with a smile, 'is the only thing I ever look at in this place, and the only one I have seen for ten years. Monsieur Prudhomme declared: "This sabre is the finest day of my life!" As for me, I can say: "This pin is the whole of my life!"'

I sought for the conventional phrase; I ended by saying: 'Some woman has made you suffer?'

He went on harshly: 'I suffer yet, and frightfully... But come on to my balcony. A name came to my lips just now, that I dared not utter, because if you had answered "dead," as you did for Sophie Astier, I should have blown out my brains, this very day.'

We had gone out on to a wide balcony looking towards two deep valleys, one on the right and the other on the left, shut in by high sombre mountains. It was that twilight hour when the vanished sun lights the earth only by its reflection in the sky.

He continued: 'Is Jeanne de Limours still alive?'

His eye was fixed on mine, full of shuddering terror.

I smiled.

'Very much alive...and prettier than ever.'

'You know her?'

'Yes.'

He hesitated: 'Intimately?'

'No.'

He took my hand: 'Talk to me about her.'

'But there is nothing I can say: she is one of the women, or rather one of the most charming and expensive gay ladies in Paris. She leads a pleasant and sumptuous life, and that's all one can say.'

He murmured: 'I love her,' as if he had said: 'I am dying.' Then abruptly: 'Ah, for three years, what a distracting and glorious life we lived! Five or six times I all but killed her; she tried to pierce my eyes with that pin at which you have been looking. There, look at this little white speck on my left eye. We loved each other! How can I explain such a passion? You would not understand it.

'There must be a gentle love, born of the swift mutual union of two hearts and two souls; but assuredly there exists a savage love, cruelly tormenting, born of the imperious force which binds together two discordant beings who adore while they hate.

'That girl ruined me in three years. I had four millions which she devoured quite placidly, in her indifferent fashion, crunching them up with a sweet smile that seemed to die from her eyes on to her lips.

'You know her? There is something irresistible about her. What is it? I don't know. Is it those grey eyes whose glance thrusts like a gimlet and remains in you like the barb of an arrow? It is rather that sweet smile, indifferent and infinitely charming, that dwells on her face like a mask. Little by little, her slow grace invades one, rises from her like a perfume, from her tall, slender body, which sways a little as she moves, for she seems to glide rather than walk, from her lovely, drawling voice that seems the music of her smile, from the very motion of her body, too, a motion that is always restrained, always just right, taking the eye with rapture, so exquisitely proportioned it is. For three years I was conscious of no one but her. How I suffered! For she deceived me with every one. Why? For no reason, for the mere sake of deceiving. And when I discovered it, when I abused her as a light-o'-love and a loose woman, she admitted it calmly. "We're not married, are we?"' she said.

'Since I have been here, I have thought of her so much that I have ended by understanding her: that woman is Manon Lescaut come again. Manon could not love without betraying for Manon, love, pleasure, and money were all one.'

He was silent. Then, some minutes later:

'When I had squandered my last sou for her, she said to me quite simply: "You realize, my dear, that I cannot live on air and sunshine. I love you madly, I love you more than anyone in the world, but one must live. Poverty and I would never make good bedfellows."'

'And if I did but tell you what an agonizing life I had led with her! When I looked at her, I wanted to kill her as sharply as I wanted to embrace her. When I looked at her...I felt a mad impulse to open my arms, to take her to me and strangle her. There lurked in her, behind her eyes, something treacherous and forever unattainable that made me execrate her; and it is perhaps because of that that I loved her so. In her, the Feminine, the detestable and distracting Feminine, was more puissant than in any other woman. She was charged with it, surcharged as with an intoxicating and venomous fluid. She was Woman, more essentially than any one woman has ever been.

'And look you, when I went out with her, she fixed her glance on every man, in such a way that she seemed to be giving each one of them her undivided interest. That maddened me and yet held me to her the closer. This woman, in the mere act of walking down the street, was owned by every man in it, in spite of me, in spite of herself, by virtue of her very nature, although she bore herself with a quiet and modest air. Do you understand?

'And what torture! At the theatre, in the restaurant, it seemed to me that men possessed her under my very eyes. And as soon as I left her company, other men did indeed possess her.

'It is ten years since I have seen her, and I love her more then ever.'

Night had spread its wings upon the earth. The powerful scent of orange-trees hung in the air.

I said to him: 'You will see her again?'

He answered: 'By God, yes. I have here, in land and money, from seven to eight hundred thousand francs. When the million is complete, I shall sell all and depart. I shall have enough for one year with her—one entire marvellous year. And then good-bye, my life will be over.'

I asked: 'But afterwards?'

'Afterwards, I don't know. It will be the end. Perhaps I shall ask her to keep me on as her body-servant.'

8

THE HAND

All were crowding around M. Bermutier, the judge, who was giving his opinion about the Saint-Cloud mystery. For a month, this inexplicable crime had been the talk of Paris. Nobody could make head or tail of it.

M. Bermutier, standing with his back to the fireplace, was talking, citing the evidence, discussing the various theories, but arriving at no conclusion.

Some women had risen, in order to get nearer to him, and were standing with their eyes fastened on the clean-shaven face of the judge, who was saying such weighty things. They were shaking and trembling, moved by fear and curiosity, and by the eager and insatiable desire for the horrible, which haunts the soul of every woman. One of them, paler than the others, said during a pause:

'It's terrible. It verges on the supernatural. The truth will never be known.'

The judge turned to her:

'True, madame, it is likely that the actual facts will never be discovered. As for the word "supernatural" which you have just used, it has nothing to do with the matter. We are in the presence of a very cleverly conceived and executed crime, so well enshrouded in mystery that we cannot disentangle it from the involved circumstances which surround it. But once, I had to take charge of an affair in which the uncanny seemed to play a part. In fact, the case became so confused that it had to be given up.'

Several women exclaimed at once:

'Oh! Tell us about it!'

M. Bermutier smiled in a dignified manner, as a judge should, and went on:

'Do not think, however, that I, for one minute, ascribed anything in the case to supernatural influences. I believe only in normal causes. But if, instead of using the word "supernatural" to express what we do not understand, we were simply to make use of the word "inexplicable," it would be much better. At any rate, in the affair of which I am about to tell you, it is especially the surrounding, preliminary circumstances which impressed me. Here are the facts:

'I was, at that time, a judge at Ajaccio, a little white city on the edge of a bay which is surrounded by high mountains.

'The majority of the cases which came up before me concerned vendettas. There are some that are superb, dramatic, ferocious, heroic. We find there the most beautiful causes for revenge of which one could dream, enmities hundreds of years old, quieted for a time but never extinguished; abominable stratagems, murders becoming massacres and almost deeds of glory. For two years I heard of nothing but the price of blood, of this terrible Corsican prejudice which compels revenge for insults meted out to the offending person and all his descendants and relatives. I had seen old men, children, cousins murdered; my head was full of these stories.

'One day I learned that an Englishman had just hired a little villa at the end of the bay for several years. He had brought with him a French servant, whom he had engaged on the way at Marseilles.

'Soon this peculiar person, living alone, only going out to hunt and fish, aroused a widespread interest. He never spoke to any one, never went to the town, and every morning he would practice for an hour or so with his revolver and rifle.

'Legends were built up around him. It was said that he was some high personage, fleeing from his fatherland for political reasons; then it was affirmed that he was in hiding after having committed some abominable crime. Some particularly horrible circumstances were even mentioned.

'In my judicial position I thought it necessary to get some information about this man, but it was impossible to learn anything. He called himself Sir John Rowell.

'I therefore had to be satisfied with watching him as closely as I could, but I could see nothing suspicious about his actions.

'However, as rumours about him were growing and becoming more widespread, I decided to try to see this stranger myself, and I began to hunt regularly in the neighborhood of his grounds.

'For a long time I watched without finding an opportunity. At last it came to me in the shape of a partridge which I shot and killed right in front of the Englishman. My dog fetched it for me, but, taking the bird, I went at once to Sir John Rowell and, begging his pardon, asked him to accept it.

'He was a big man, with red hair and beard, very tall, very broad, a kind of calm and polite Hercules. He had nothing of the so-called British stiffness, and in a broad English accent he thanked me warmly for my attention. At the end of a month we had had five or six conversations.

'One night, at last, as I was passing before his door, I saw him in the garden, seated astride a chair, smoking his pipe. I bowed and he invited me to come in and have a glass of beer. I needed no urging.

'He received me with the most punctilious English courtesy, sang the praises of France and of Corsica, and declared that he was quite in love with this country.

'Then, with great caution and under the guise of a vivid

interest, I asked him a few questions about his life and his plans. He answered without embarrassment, telling me that he had travelled a great deal in Africa, in the Indies, in America. He added, laughing:

"I have had many adventures."

'Then I turned the conversation on hunting, and he gave me the most curious details on hunting the hippopotamus, the tiger, the elephant and even the gorilla.

'I said:

"Are all these animals dangerous?"

'He smiled:

"Oh, no! Man is the worst."

'And he laughed a good broad laugh, the wholesome laugh of a contented Englishman.

"I have also frequently been man-hunting."

'Then he began to talk about weapons, and he invited me to come in and see different makes of guns.

'His parlor was draped in black, black silk embroidered in gold. Big yellow flowers, as brilliant as fire, were worked on the dark material.

'He said:

"It is a Japanese material."

'But in the middle of the widest panel a strange thing attracted my attention. A black object stood out against a square of red velvet. I went up to it; it was a hand, a human hand. Not the clean white hand of a skeleton, but a dried black hand, with yellow nails, the muscles exposed and traces of old blood on the bones, which were cut off as clean as though it had been chopped off with an axe, near the middle of the forearm.

'Around the wrist, an enormous iron chain, riveted and soldered to this unclean member, fastened it to the wall by a ring, strong enough to hold an elephant in leash.

'I asked:

"What is that?"

'The Englishman answered quietly:

"That is my best enemy. It comes from America, too. The bones were severed by a sword and the skin cut off with a sharp stone and dried in the sun for a week."

'I touched these human remains, which must have belonged to a giant. The uncommonly long fingers were attached by enormous tendons which still had pieces of skin hanging to them in places. This hand was terrible to see; it made one think of some savage vengeance.

'I said:

"This man must have been very strong."

'The Englishman answered quietly:

"Yes, but I was stronger than he. I put on this chain to hold him."

'I thought that he was joking. I said:

"This chain is useless now, the hand won't run away."

'Sir John Rowell answered seriously:

"It always wants to go away. This chain is needed."

'I glanced at him quickly, questioning his face, and I asked myself:

"Is he an insane man or a practical joker?"

'But his face remained inscrutable, calm and friendly. I turned to other subjects, and admired his rifles.

'However, I noticed that he kept three loaded revolvers in the room, as though constantly in fear of some attack.

'I paid him several calls. Then I did not go any more. People had become used to his presence; everybody had lost interest in him.

'A whole year rolled by. One morning, toward the end of November, my servant awoke me and announced that Sir John Rowell had been murdered during the night.

'Half an hour later I entered the Englishman's house, together with the police commissioner and the captain of the gendarmes.

The servant, bewildered and in despair, was crying before the door. At first, I suspected this man, but he was innocent.

'The guilty party could never be found.

'On entering Sir John's parlor, I noticed the body, stretched out on its back, in the middle of the room.

'His vest was torn, the sleeve of his jacket had been pulled off, everything pointed to, a violent struggle.

'The Englishman had been strangled! His face was black, swollen and frightful, and seemed to express a terrible fear. He held something between his teeth, and his neck, pierced by five or six holes which looked as though they had been made by some iron instrument, was covered with blood.

'A physician joined us. He examined the finger marks on the neck for a long time and then made this strange announcement:

"It looks as though he had been strangled by a skeleton."

'A cold chill seemed to run down my back, and I looked over to where I had formerly seen the terrible hand. It was no longer there. The chain was hanging down, broken.

'I bent over the dead man and, in his contracted mouth, I found one of the fingers of this vanished hand, cut — or rather sawed off by the teeth down to the second knuckle.

'Then the investigation began. Nothing could be discovered. No door, window or piece of furniture had been forced. The two watch dogs had not been aroused from their sleep.

'Here, in a few words, is the testimony of the servant:

'For a month his master had seemed excited. He had received many letters, which he would immediately burn.

'Often, in a fit of passion which approached madness, he had taken a switch and struck wildly at this dried hand riveted to the wall, and which had disappeared, no one knows how, at the very hour of the crime.

'He would go to bed very late and carefully lock himself in. He always kept weapons within reach. Often at night he would talk loudly, as though he were quarrelling with some one.

'That night, somehow, he had made no noise, and it was only on going to open the windows that the servant had found Sir John murdered. He suspected no one.

'I communicated what I knew of the dead man to the judges and public officials. Throughout the whole island a minute investigation was carried on. Nothing could be found out.

'One night, about three months after the crime, I had a terrible nightmare. I seemed to see the horrible hand running over my curtains and walls like an immense scorpion or spider. Three times I awoke, three times I went to sleep again; three times I saw the hideous object galloping round my room and moving its fingers like legs.

'The following day the hand was brought me, found in the cemetery, on the grave of Sir John Rowell, who had been buried there because we had been unable to find his family. The first finger was missing.

'Ladies, there is my story. I know nothing more.'

The women, deeply stirred, were pale and trembling. One of them exclaimed:

'But that is neither a climax nor an explanation! We will be unable to sleep unless you give us your opinion of what had occurred.'

The judge smiled severely:

'Oh! Ladies, I shall certainly spoil your terrible dreams. I simply believe that the legitimate owner of the hand was not dead, that he came to get it with his remaining one. But I don't know how. It was a kind of vendetta.'

One of the women murmured:

'No, it can't be that.'

And the judge, still smiling, said:

'Didn't I tell you that my explanation would not satisfy you?'

9

IN THE WOOD

As the mayor was about to sit down to breakfast, word was brought to him that the rural policeman, with two prisoners, was awaiting him at the Hotel de Ville. He went there at once and found old Hochedur standing guard before a middle-class couple whom he was regarding with a severe expression on his face.

The man, a fat old fellow with a red nose and white hair, seemed utterly dejected; while the woman, a little roundabout individual with shining cheeks, looked at the official who had arrested them, with defiant eyes.

'What is it? What is it, Hochedur?'

The rural policeman made his deposition: He had gone out that morning at his usual time, in order to patrol his beat from the forest of Champioux as far as the boundaries of Argenteuil. He had not noticed anything unusual in the country except that it was a fine day, and that the wheat was doing well, when the son of old Bredel, who was going over his vines, called out to him: 'Here, Daddy Hochedur, go and have a look at the outskirts of the wood. In the first thicket you will find a pair of pigeons who must be a hundred and thirty years old between them!'

He went in the direction indicated, entered the thicket, and there he heard words which made him suspect a flagrant breach of morality. Advancing, therefore, on his hands and knees as if to surprise a poacher, he had arrested the couple whom he found there.

The mayor looked at the culprits in astonishment, for the man was certainly sixty, and the woman fifty-five at least, and he began to question them, beginning with the man, who replied in such a weak voice that he could scarcely be heard.

'What is your name?'

'Nicholas Beaurain.'

'Your occupation?'

'Haberdasher, in the Rue des Martyrs, in Paris.'

'What were you doing in the wood?'

The haberdasher remained silent, with his eyes on his fat paunch, and his hands hanging at his sides, and the mayor continued:

'Do you deny what the officer of the municipal authorities states?'

'No, monsieur.'

'So you confess it?'

'Yes, monsieur.'

'What have you to say in your defence?'

'Nothing, monsieur.'

'Where did you meet the partner in your misdemeanor?'

'She is my wife, monsieur.'

'Your wife?'

'Yes, monsieur.'

'Then—then—you do not live together in Paris?'

'I beg your pardon, monsieur, but we are living together!'

'But in that case—you must be mad, altogether mad, my dear sir, to get caught playing lovers in the country at ten o'clock in the morning.'

The haberdasher seemed ready to cry with shame, and he muttered: 'It was she who enticed me! I told her it was very stupid, but when a woman once gets a thing into her head—you know—

you cannot get it out.'

The mayor, who liked a joke, smiled and replied: 'In your case, the contrary ought to have happened. You would not be here, if she had had the idea only in her head.'

Then Monsieur Beaurain was seized with rage and turning to his wife, he said: 'Do you see to what you have brought us with your poetry? And now we shall have to go before the courts at our age, for a breach of morals! And we shall have to shut up the shop, sell our good will, and go to some other neighborhood! That's what it has come to.'

Madame Beaurain got up, and without looking at her husband, she explained herself without embarrassment, without useless modesty, and almost without hesitation.

'Of course, monsieur, I know that we have made ourselves ridiculous. Will you allow me to plead my cause like an advocate, or rather like a poor woman? And I hope that you will be kind enough to send us home, and to spare us the disgrace of a prosecution.

'Years ago, when I was young, I made Monsieur Beaurain's acquaintance one Sunday in this neighborhood. He was employed in a draper's shop, and I was a saleswoman in a ready-made clothing establishment. I remember it as if it were yesterday. I used to come and spend Sundays here occasionally with a friend of mine, Rose Leveque, with whom I lived in the Rue Pigalle, and Rose had a sweetheart, while I had none. He used to bring us here, and one Saturday he told me laughing that he should bring a friend with him the next day. I quite understood what he meant, but I replied that it would be no good; for I was virtuous, monsieur.

'The next day we met Monsieur Beaurain at the railway station, and in those days he was good-looking, but I had made up my mind not to encourage him, and I did not. Well, we arrived at Bezons. It was a lovely day, the sort of day that touches your heart. When it is fine even now, just as it used to be formerly, I grow quite foolish, and when I am in the country I utterly lose my head. The green grass, the swallows flying so swiftly, the smell of the grass, the scarlet poppies, the daisies, all that makes me crazy. It is like champagne when one is not accustomed to it!

'Well, it was lovely weather, warm and bright, and it seemed to penetrate your body through your eyes when you looked, and through your mouth when you breathed. Rose and Simon hugged and kissed each other every minute, and that gave me a queer feeling! Monsieur Beaurain and I walked behind them, without speaking much, for when people do not know each other, they do not find anything to talk about. He looked timid, and I liked to see his embarrassment. At last we got to the little wood; it was as cool as in a bath there, and we four sat down. Rose and her lover teased me because I looked rather stern, but you will understand that I could not be otherwise. And then they began to kiss and hug again, without putting any more restraint upon themselves than if we had not been there; and then they whispered together, and got up and went off among the trees, without saying a word. You may fancy what I looked like, alone with this young fellow whom I saw for the first time. I felt so confused at seeing them go that it gave me courage, and I began to talk. I asked him what his business was, and he said he was a linen draper's assistant, as I told you just now. We talked for a few minutes, and that made him bold, and he wanted to take liberties with me, but I told him sharply to keep his place. Is not that true, Monsieur Beaurain?'

Monsieur Beaurain, who was looking at his feet in confusion, did not reply, and she continued: 'Then he saw that I was virtuous, and he began to make love to me nicely, like an honorable man, and from that time he came every Sunday, for he was very much in love with me. I was very fond of him also, very fond of him! He was a good-looking fellow, formerly, and in short he married me the next September, and we started in business in the Rue des Martyrs.

'It was a hard struggle for some years, monsieur. Business did not prosper, and we could not afford many country excursions, and, besides, we had got out of the way of them. One has other things in one's head, and thinks more of the cash box than of pretty speeches, when one is in business. We were growing old by degrees without perceiving it, like quiet people who do not think much about love. One does not regret anything as long as one does not notice what one has lost.

'And then, monsieur, business became better, and we were tranquil as to the future! Then, you see, I do not exactly know what went on in my mind, no, I really do not know, but I began to dream like a little boarding-school girl. The sight of the little carts full of flowers which are drawn about the streets made me cry; the smell of violets sought me out in my easy-chair, behind my cash box, and made my heart beat! Then I would get up and go out on the doorstep to look at the blue sky between the roofs. When one looks up at the sky from the street, it looks like a river which is descending on Paris, winding as it flows, and the swallows pass to and fro in it like fish. These ideas are very stupid at my age! But how can one help it, monsieur, when one has worked all one's life? A moment comes in which one perceives that one could have done something else, and that one regrets, oh! Yes, one feels intense regret! Just think, for twenty years I might have gone and had kisses in the woods, like other women. I used to think how delightful it would be to lie under the trees and be in love with some one! And I thought of it every day and every night! I dreamed of the moonlight on the water, until I felt inclined to drown myself.

'I did not venture to speak to Monsieur Beaurain about this at first. I knew that he would make fun of me, and send me back to sell my needles and cotton! And then, to speak the truth, Monsieur Beaurain never said much to me, but when I looked in the glass, I also understood quite well that I no longer appealed to any one!

'Well, I made up my mind, and I proposed to him an excursion into the country, to the place where we had first become acquainted. He agreed without mistrusting anything, and we arrived here this morning, about nine o'clock.

'I felt quite young again when I got among the wheat, for a woman's heart never grows old! And really, I no longer saw my husband as he is at present, but just as he was formerly! That I will swear to you, monsieur. As true as I am standing here I was crazy. I began to kiss him, and he was more surprised than if I had tried to murder him. He kept saying to me: "Why, you must be mad! You are mad this morning! What is the matter with you?" I did not listen to him, I only listened to my own heart, and I made him come into the wood with me. That is all. I have spoken the truth, Monsieur le Maire, the whole truth.'

The mayor was a sensible man. He rose from his chair, smiled, and said: 'Go in peace, madame, and when you again visit our forests, be more discreet.'

10

OLD MONGILET

In the office, old mongilet was looked on as a 'character.' He was an old employee, a good-natured creature, who had never been outside Paris but once in his life.

It was the end of July, and we all went every Sunday to roll in the grass, or bathe in the river in the country near by. Asnieres, Argenteuil, Chatou, Bougival, Maisons, Poissy, had their habitues and their ardent admirers. We argued about the merits and advantages of all these places, celebrated and delightful to all employees in Paris.

Old Mongilet would say: 'You are like a lot of sheep! A nice place, this country you talk of!'

And we would ask: 'Well, how about you, Mongilet? Don't you ever go on an excursion?'

'Yes, indeed. I go in an omnibus. When I have had a good luncheon, without any hurry, at the wine shop below, I look up my route with a plan of Paris and the time-table of the lines and connections. And then I climb up on top of the bus, open my umbrella and off we go. Oh, I see lots of things, more than you, I bet! I change my surroundings. It is as though I were taking a journey across the world, the people are so different in one street and another. I know my Paris better than anyone. And then, there is nothing more amusing than the entresols. You would not believe what one sees in there at a glance. One can guess a domestic scene simply by seeing the face of a man shouting; one is amused on passing by a barber's shop to see the barber leave his customer all covered with lather to look out in the street. One exchanges heartfelt glances with the milliners just for fun, as one has no time to alight. Ah, how many things one sees!

'It is the drama, real, true, natural drama that one sees as the horses trot by. Heavens! I would not give my excursions in the omnibus for all your stupid excursions in the woods.'

'Come and try it, Mongilet, come to the country once just to see.'

'I was there once,' he replied, 'twenty years ago, and you will never catch me there again.'

'Tell us about it, Mongilet.'

'If you wish to hear it. This is how it was: You knew Boivin, the old clerk, whom we called Boileau?'

'Yes, perfectly.'

'He was my office chum. The rascal had a house at Colombes and always invited me to spend Sunday with him. He would say: "Come alone, Maculotte (he called me Maculotte for fun). You will see what a nice walk we shall take."'

'I let myself be trapped like an animal, and set out one morning by the eight o'clock train. I arrived at a kind of town, a country town where there is nothing to see, and I at length found my way to an old wooden door with an iron bell, at the end of an alley between two walls.

'I rang, and waited a long time, and at last the door was opened. What was it that opened it? I could not tell at the first glance. A woman or an ape? The creature was old, ugly, covered with old clothes that looked dirty and wicked. It had chickens' feathers in its hair and looked as though it would devour me.

"What do you want?" she said.

"M. Boivin."

"What do you want of him, of M. Boivin?"

'I felt ill at ease on being questioned by this fury. I stammered: "Why—he expects me."

"Ah, it is you who are coming to lunch?"

"Yes," I stammered, trembling.

'Then, turning toward the house, she cried in an angry tone: "Boivin, here is your man!"

'It was my friend's wife. Little Boivin appeared immediately on the threshold of a sort of barrack of plaster covered with zinc, that looked like a foot-warmer. He wore white duck trousers covered with stains and a dirty Panama-hat.

'After shaking my hands warmly, he took me into what he called his garden. It was at the end of another alleyway enclosed by high walls and was a little square the size of a pocket-handkerchief, surrounded by houses that were so high that the sun could reach it only two or three hours in the day. Pansies, pinks, wallflowers and a few rose bushes were languishing in this airless well which was as hot as an oven from the refraction of heat from the roofs.

"I have no trees," said Boivin, "but the neighbours' walls take their place. I have as much shade as in a wood."'

'Then he took hold of a button of my coat and said in a low tone:

"You can do me a service. You saw the wife. She is not agreeable, eh? Today, as I had invited you, she gave me clean clothes; but if I spot them all is lost. I counted on you to water my plants."'

'I agreed. I took off my coat, rolled up my sleeves, and began to work the handle of a kind of pump that wheezed, puffed and rattled like a consumptive as it emitted a thread of water like a Wallace drinking-fountain. It took me ten minutes to fill the watering-pot, and I was in a bath of perspiration. Boivin directed me:

"Here—this plant—a little more; enough—now this one."'

'The watering-pot leaked and my feet got more water than the flowers. The bottoms of my trousers were soaking and covered with mud. And twenty times running I kept it up, soaking my feet afresh each time, and perspiring anew as I worked the handle of the pump. And when I was tired out and wanted to stop, Boivin, in a tone of entreaty, said as he put his hand on my arm:

"Just one more watering-potful—just one, and that will be all."'

'To thank me he gave me a rose, a big rose, but hardly had it touched my buttonhole than it fell to pieces, leaving of my decoration only a hard little green knot. I was surprised, but said nothing.

'Mme Boivin's voice was heard in the distance: "'Are you ever coming? I tell you lunch is ready!"'

'We went towards the foot-warmer. If the garden was in the shade, the house, on the other hand, was in the blazing sun, and the sweating-room of a Turkish bath is not so hot as my friend's dining-room was.

'Three plates, at the side of which were some half-washed forks, were placed in a table of yellow wood. In the middle stood an earthenware dish containing warmed-up boiled beef and potatoes. We began to eat.

'A large water-bottle full of water lightly coloured with wine attracted my attention. Boivin, embarrassed, said to his wife:

"See here, my dear, just on a special occasion, are you not going to give us a little undiluted wine?"'

'She looked at him furiously.

"So that you may both get tipsy, is that it, and stay here gabbing all day? A fine special occasion!"'

'He said no more. After the stew she brought in another dish of potatoes cooked with bacon. When this dish was finished, still in silence, she announced:

"That is all! Now get out!"'

'Boivin looked at her in astonishment.

"But the pigeon—the pigeon you plucked this morning?"'

'She put her hands on her hips:

"Perhaps you have not had enough? Because you bring people here is no reason why we should devour all that there is in the house. What is there for me to eat this evening?"'

'We rose. Boivin whispered:

"Wait for me a second, and we will skip."

'He went into the kitchen where his wife had gone, and I overheard him say:

"Give me twenty sous, my dear."

"What do you want with twenty sous?"

"Why, one does not know what may happen. It is always better to have some money."

'She yelled so that I should hear:

"No, I will not give it to you!

As the man has had luncheon here, the least he can do is to pay your expenses for the day."

'Boivin came back to fetch me. As I wished to be polite I bowed to the mistress of the house, stammering:

"Madame—many thanks—kind welcome."

"That's all right," she replied. "But do not bring him back drunk, for you will have to answer to me, you know!"

'We set out. We had to cross a perfectly bare plain under the burning sun. I attempted to gather a flower along the road and gave a cry of pain. It had hurt my hand frightfully. They call these plants nettles. And, everywhere, there was a smell of manure, enough to turn your stomach.

'Boivin said, "Have a little patience and we will reach the river bank."

'We reached the river. Here there was an odour of mud and dirty water, and the sun blazed down on the water so that it burned my eyes. I begged Boivin to go under cover somewhere. He took me into a kind of shanty filled with men, a river boatmen's tavern.

'He said: "This does not look very grand, but it is very comfortable."

'I was hungry. I ordered an omelet. But lo and behold, at the second glass of wine, that cursed Boivin lost his head, and I understand why his wife gave him water in his wine.

'He got up, declaimed, wanted to show his strength, interfered in a quarrel between two drunken men who were fighting, and, but for the landlord, who came to the rescue, we should both have been killed.

'I dragged him away, holding him up until we reached the first bush, where I deposited him. I lay down beside him and apparently I fell asleep. We must certainly have slept a long time, for it was dark when I awoke. Boivin was snoring at my side. I shook him; he rose, but he was still drunk, though a little less so.

'We set out through the darkness across the plain. Boivin said he knew the way. He made me turn to the left, then to the right, then to the left. We could see neither sky nor earth, and found ourselves lost in the midst of a kind of forest of wooden stakes, that came as high as our noses. It was a vineyard and these were the supports. There was not a single light on the horizon. We wandered about in this vineyard for about an hour or two, hesitating, reaching out our arms without coming to the end, for we kept retracing our steps.

'At length Boivin fell against a stake that tore his cheek and he remained in a sitting posture on the ground, uttering with all his might long and resounding hellos, while I screamed "Help! Help!" as loud as I could, lighting wax-matches to show the way to our rescuers, and also to keep up my courage.

'At last, a belated peasant heard us and put us on our right road. I took Boivin to his home, but as I was leaving him on the threshold of his garden, the door opened suddenly and his wife appeared, a candle in her hand. She frightened me horribly.

'As soon as she saw her husband, whom she must have been waiting for since dark, she screamed, as she darted toward me:

"Ah, scoundrel, I knew you would bring him back drunk!"

'My, how I made my escape, running all the way to the station, and as I thought the fury was pursuing me I shut myself in an inner room, as the train was not due for half an hour.

'That is why I never married, and why I never go out of Paris.'

11

A PIECE OF STRING

It was market-day, and from all the country round Goderville the peasants and their wives were coming toward the town. The men walked slowly, throwing the whole body forward at every step of their long, crooked legs. They were deformed from pushing the plough which makes the left-shoulder higher, and bends their figures side-ways; from reaping the grain, when they have to spread their legs so as to keep on their feet. Their starched blue blouses, glossy as though varnished, ornamented at collar and cuffs with a little embroidered design and blown out around their bony bodies, looked very much like balloons about to soar, whence issued two arms and two feet.

Some of these fellows dragged a cow or a calf at the end of a rope. And just behind the animal followed their wives beating it over the back with a leaf-covered branch to hasten its pace, and carrying large baskets out of which protruded the heads of chickens or ducks. These women walked more quickly and energetically than the men, with their erect, dried-up figures, adorned with scanty little shawls pinned over their flat bosoms, and their heads wrapped round with a white cloth, enclosing the hair and surmounted by a cap.

Now a char-a-banc passed by, jogging along behind a nag and shaking up strangely the two men on the seat, and the woman at the bottom of the cart who held fast to its sides to lessen the hard jolting.

In the market-place at Goderville was a great crowd, a mingled multitude of men and beasts. The horns of cattle, the high, long-napped hats of wealthy peasants, the headdresses of the women came to the surface of that sea. And the sharp, shrill, barking voices made a continuous, wild din, while above it occasionally rose a huge burst of laughter from the sturdy lungs of a merry peasant or a prolonged bellow from a cow tied fast to the wall of a house.

It all smelled of the stable, of milk, of hay and of perspiration, giving off that half-human, half-animal odour which is peculiar to country folks.

Maitre Hauchecorne, of Breaute, had just arrived at Goderville and was making his way toward the square when he perceived on the ground a little piece of string. Maitre Hauchecorne, economical as are all true Normans, reflected that everything was worth picking up which could be of any use, and he stooped down, but painfully, because he suffered from rheumatism. He took the bit of thin string from the ground and was carefully preparing to roll it up when he saw Maitre Malandain, the harness maker, on his doorstep staring at him. They had once had a quarrel about a halter, and they had borne each other malice ever since. Maitre Hauchecorne was overcome with a sort of shame at being seen by his enemy picking up a bit of string in the road. He quickly hid it beneath his blouse and then slipped it into his breeches, pocket, then pretended to be still looking for something on the ground which he did not discover and finally went off toward the market-place, his head bent forward and his body almost doubled in two by rheumatic pains.

He was at once lost in the crowd, which kept moving about slowly and noisily as it chaffered and bargained. The peasants examined the cows, went off, came back, always in doubt for fear of being cheated, never quite daring to decide, looking the seller square in the eye in the effort to discover the tricks of the man and the defect in the beast.

The women, having placed their great baskets at their feet, had taken out the poultry, which lay upon the ground, their legs tied together, with terrified eyes and scarlet combs.

They listened to propositions, maintaining their prices in a decided manner with an impassive face or perhaps deciding to accept the smaller price offered, suddenly calling out to the customer who was starting to go away: 'All right, I'll let you have them, Mait' Anthime.'

Then, little by little, the square became empty, and when the Angelus struck midday, those who lived at a distance poured into the inns.

At Jourdain's, the great room was filled with eaters, just as the vast court was filled with vehicles of every sort—wagons, gigs, chars-a- bancs, tilburies, innumerable vehicles which have no name, yellow with mud, misshapen, pieced together, raising their shafts to heaven like two arms, or it may be with their nose on the ground and their rear in the air.

Just opposite to where the diners were at table, the huge fireplace, with its bright flame, gave out a burning heat on the backs of those who sat at the right. Three spits were turning, loaded with chickens, with pigeons and with joints of mutton, and a delectable odour of roast meat and of gravy flowing over crisp brown skin arose from the hearth, kindled merriment, caused mouths to water.

All the aristocracy of the plough were eating there at Mait' Jourdain's, the innkeeper's, a dealer in horses also and a sharp fellow who had made a great deal of money in his day.

The dishes were passed round, were emptied, as were the jugs of yellow cider. Every one told of his affairs, of his purchases and his sales. They exchanged news about the crops. The weather was good for greens, but too wet for grain.

Suddenly the drum began to beat in the courtyard before the house. Every one, except some of the most indifferent, was on their feet at once and ran to the door, to the windows, their mouths full and napkins in their hand.

When the public crier had finished his tattoo he called forth in a jerky voice, pausing in the wrong places: 'Be it known to the inhabitants of Goderville and in general to all persons present at the market that there has been lost this morning on the Beuzeville road, between nine and ten o'clock, a black leather pocketbook containing five hundred francs and business papers. You are requested to return it to the mayor's office at once or to Maitre Fortune Houlbreque, of Manneville. There will be twenty francs reward.'

Then the man went away. They heard once more at a distance the dull beating of the drum and the faint voice of the crier. Then they all began to talk of this incident, reckoning up the chances which Maitre Houlbreque had of finding or of not finding his pocketbook again.

The meal went on. They were finishing their coffee when the corporal of gendarmes appeared on the threshold.

He asked: 'Is Maitre Hauchecorne, of Breaute, here?'

Maitre Hauchecorne, seated at the other end of the table answered: 'Here I am, here I am.'

And he followed the corporal.

The mayor was waiting for him, seated in an armchair. He was the notary of the place, a tall, grave man of pompous speech.

'Maitre Hauchecorne,' said he, 'this morning on the Beuzeville road, you were seen to pick up the pocketbook lost by Maitre Houlbreque, of Manneville.'

The countryman looked at the mayor in amazement, frightened already at this suspicion which rested on him, he knew not why.

'I — I picked up that pocketbook?'

'Yes, YOU.'

'I swear I don't even know anything about it.'

'You were seen.'

'I was seen — I? Who saw me?'

'M. Malandain, the harness-maker.'

Then the old man remembered, understood, and, reddening with anger, said: 'Ah! he saw me, did he, the rascal? He saw me picking up this string here, M'sieu le Maire.'

And fumbling at the bottom of his pocket, he pulled out of it the little end of string.

But the mayor incredulously shook his head: 'You will not make me believe, Maitre Hauchecorne, that M. Malandain, who is a man whose word can be relied on, has mistaken this string for a pocketbook.'

The peasant, furious, raised his hand and spat on the ground beside him as if to attest his good faith, repeating: 'For all that, it is God's truth, M'sieu le Maire. There! On my soul's salvation, I repeat it.'

The mayor continued: 'After you picked up the object in question, you even looked about for some time in the mud to see if a piece of money had not dropped out of it.'

The good man was choking with indignation and fear.

'How can they tell — how can they tell such lies as that to slander an honest man! How can they?'

His protestations were in vain; he was not believed.

He was confronted with M. Malandain, who repeated and sustained his testimony. They railed at one another for an hour. At his own request Maitre Hauchecorne was searched. Nothing was found on him.

At last the mayor, much perplexed, sent him away, warning him that he would inform the public prosecutor and ask for orders.

The news had spread. When he left the mayor's office the

old man was surrounded, interrogated with a curiosity which was serious or mocking, as the case might be, but into which no indignation entered. And he began to tell the story of the string. They did not believe him. They laughed.

He passed on, buttonholed by every one, himself buttonholing his acquaintances, beginning over and over again his tale and his protestations, showing his pockets turned inside out to prove that he had nothing in them.

They said to him: 'You old rogue!'

He grew more and more angry, feverish, in despair at not being believed, and kept on telling his story.

The night came. It was time to go home. He left with three of his neighbors, to whom he pointed out the place where he had picked up the string, and all the way he talked of his adventure.

That evening, he made the round of the village of Breaute for the purpose of telling everyone. He met only unbelievers.

He brooded over it all night long.

The next day, about one in the afternoon, Marius Paumelle, a farm hand of Maitre Breton, the market gardener at Ymauville, returned the pocketbook and its contents to Maitre Holbreque, of Manneville.

This man said, indeed, that he had found it on the road, but not knowing how to read, he had carried it home and given it to his master.

The news spread to the environs. Maitre Hauchecorne was informed. He started off at once and began to relate his story with the denouement. He was triumphant.

'What grieved me,' said he, 'was not the thing itself, do you understand, but it was being accused of lying. Nothing does you so much harm as being in disgrace for lying.'

All day he talked of his adventure. He told it on the roads to the people who passed, at the cabaret to the people who drank and next Sunday when they came out of church. He even stopped strangers to tell them about it. He was easy now, and yet something worried him without his knowing exactly what it was. People had a joking manner while they listened. They did not seem convinced. He seemed to feel their remarks behind his back.

On Tuesday of the following week he went to market at Goderville, prompted solely by the need of telling his story.

Malandain, standing on his doorstep, began to laugh as he saw him pass. Why?

He accosted a farmer of Criquetot, who did not let him finish, and giving him a punch in the pit of the stomach cried in his face: 'Oh, you great rogue!' Then he turned his heel upon him.

Maitre Hauchecorne remained speechless and grew more and more uneasy. Why had they called him 'great rogue'?

When seated at table in Jourdain's tavern, he began again to explain the whole affair.

A horse dealer of Montivilliers shouted at him:

'Get out, get out, you old scamp! I know all about your old string.'

Hauchecorne stammered:

'But since they found it again, the pocketbook!'

But the other continued:

'Hold your tongue, daddy; there's one who finds it and there's another who returns it. And no one the wiser.'

The farmer was speechless. He understood at last. They accused him of having had the pocketbook brought back by an accomplice, by a confederate.

He tried to protest. The whole table began to laugh.

He could not finish his dinner, and went away amid a chorus of jeers.

He went home indignant, choking with rage, with confusion, the more cast down since with his Norman craftiness he was, perhaps, capable of having done what they accused him of and even of boasting of it as a good trick. He was dimly conscious that it was impossible to prove his innocence, his craftiness being so well known. He felt himself struck to the heart by the injustice of the suspicion.

He began anew to tell his tale, lengthening his recital every day, each day adding new proofs, more energetic declarations and more sacred oaths, which he thought of, which he prepared in his hours of solitude, for his mind was entirely occupied with the story of the string. The more he denied it, the more artful his arguments, the less he was believed.

'Those are liars' proofs,' they said behind his back.

He felt this. It preyed upon him and he exhausted himself in useless efforts.

He was visibly wasting away.

Jokers would make him tell the story of 'the piece of string' to amuse them, just as you make a soldier who has been on a campaign tell his story of the battle. His mind kept growing weaker and about the end of December he took to his bed.

He passed away early in January, and, in the ravings of death agony, he protested his innocence, repeating:

'A little bit of string—a little bit of string. See, here it is, M'sieu le Maire.'

12

TIMBUCTOO

The boulevard, that river of humanity, was alive with people in the golden light of the setting sun. The whole sky was red, blinding, and behind the Madeleine an immense bank of flaming clouds cast a shower of light the whole length of tile boulevard, vibrant as the heat from a brazier.

The gay, animated crowd went by in this golden mist and seemed to be glorified. Their faces were gilded, their black hats and clothes took on purple tints, the patent leather of their shoes cast bright reflections on the asphalt of the sidewalk.

Before the cafes, a mass of men were drinking opalescent liquids that looked like precious stones dissolved in the glasses.

In the midst of the drinkers two officers in full uniform dazzled all eyes with their glittering gold lace. They chatted, happy without asking why, in this glory of life, in this radiant light of sunset, and they looked at the crowd, the leisurely men and the hurrying women who left a bewildering odor of perfume as they passed by.

All at once an enormous negro, dressed in black, with a paunch beneath his jean waistcoat, which was covered with charms, his face shining as if it had been polished, passed before them with a triumphant air. He laughed at the passers-by, at the news vendors, at the dazzling sky, at the whole of Paris. He was so tall that he overtopped everyone else, and when he passed, all the loungers turned round to look at his back.

But he suddenly perceived the officers and darted towards them, jostling the drinkers in his path. As soon as he reached their table, he fixed his gleaming and delighted eyes upon them and the corners of his mouth expanded to his ears, showing his dazzling white teeth like a crescent moon in a black sky. The two men looked in astonishment at this ebony giant, unable to understand his delight.

With a voice that made all the guests laugh, he said:

'Good-day, my lieutenant.'

One of the officers was commander of a battalion, the other was a colonel. The former said:

'I do not know you, sir. I am at a loss to know what you want of me.'

'Me like you much, Lieutenant Vedie, siege of Bezi, much grapes, find me.'

The officer, utterly bewildered, looked at the man intently, trying to refresh his memory. Then he cried abruptly:

'Timbuctoo?'

The negro, radiant, slapped his thigh as he uttered a tremendous laugh and roared:

'Yes, yes, my lieutenant; you remember Timbuctoo, ya. How do you do?'

The commandant held out his hand, laughing heartily as he did so. Then Timbuctoo became serious. He seized the officer's hand and, before the other could prevent it, he kissed it, according to negro and Arab custom. The officer embarrassed, said in a severe tone:

'Come now, Timbuctoo, we are not in Africa. Sit down there and tell me how it is I find you here.'

Timbuctoo swelled himself out and, his words falling over one another, replied hurriedly:

'Make much money, much, big restaurant, good food; Prussians, me, much steal, much, French cooking; Timbuctoo cook to the emperor; two thousand francs mine. Ha, ha, ha, ha!'

And he laughed, doubling himself up, roaring, with wild delight in his glances.

When the officer, who understood his strange manner of expressing himself, had questioned him he said:

'Well, au revoir, Timbuctoo. I will see you again.'

The negro rose, this time shaking the hand that was extended to him and, smiling still, cried:

'Good-day, good-day, my lieutenant!'

He went off so happy that he gesticulated as he walked, and people thought he was crazy.

'Who is that brute?' asked the colonel.

'A fine fellow and a brave soldier. I will tell you what I know about him. It is funny enough.

'You know that at the commencement of the war of 1870, I was shut up in Bezieres, that this negro calls Bezi. We were not besieged, but blockaded. The Prussian lines surrounded us on all sides, outside the reach of cannon, not firing on us, but slowly starving us out.

'I was then lieutenant. Our garrison consisted of soldiers of all descriptions, fragments of slaughtered regiments, some that had run away, freebooters separated from the main army, etc. We had all kinds, in fact even eleven Turcos [Algerian soldiers in the service of France], who arrived one evening no one knew whence or how. They appeared at the gates of the city, exhausted, in rags, starving and dirty. They were handed over to me.

'I saw very soon that they were absolutely undisciplined, always in the street and always drunk. I tried putting them in the police station, even in prison, but nothing was of any use. They would disappear, sometimes for days at a time, as if they had been swallowed up by the earth, and then come back staggering drunk. They had no money. Where did they buy drink and how and with what?

'This began to worry me greatly, all the more as these savages interested me with their everlasting laugh and their characteristics of overgrown frolicsome children.

'I then noticed that they blindly obeyed the largest among them, the one you have just seen. He made them do as he pleased, planned their mysterious expeditions with the all-powerful and undisputed authority of a leader. I sent for him and questioned him. Our conversation lasted fully three hours, for it was hard for me to understand his remarkable gibberish. As for him, poor devil, he made unheard-of efforts to make himself intelligible, invented words, gesticulated, perspired in his anxiety, mopping his forehead, puffing, stopping and abruptly beginning again when he thought he had found a new method of explaining what he wanted to say.

'I gathered finally that he was the son of a big chief, a sort of negro king of the region around Timbuctoo. I asked him his name. He repeated something like "Chavaharibouhalikranafotapolara." It seemed simpler to me to give him the name of his native place, "Timbuctoo." And a week later he was known by no other name in the garrison.

'But we were all wildly anxious to find out where this African ex-prince procured his drinks. I discovered it in a singular manner.

'I was on the ramparts one morning, watching the horizon, when I perceived something moving about in a vineyard. It was near the time of vintage, the grapes were ripe, but I was not thinking of that. I thought that a spy was approaching the town, and I organized a complete expedition to catch the prowler. I took command myself, after obtaining permission from the general.

'I sent out by three different gates three little companies, which were to meet at the suspected vineyard and form a cordon round it. In order to cut off the spy's retreat, one of these detachments had to make at least an hour's march. A watch on the walls signalled to me that the person I had seen had not left the place. We went along in profound silence, creeping, almost crawling, along the ditches. At last we reached the spot assigned.

'I abruptly disbanded my soldiers, who darted into the vineyard and found Timbuctoo on hands and knees travelling around among the vines and eating grapes, or rather devouring them as a dog eats his sop, snatching them in mouthfuls from the vine with his teeth.

'I wanted him to get up, but he could not think of it. I then understood why he was crawling on his hands and knees. As soon as we stood him on his feet, he began to wabble, then stretched out his arms and fell down on his nose. He was more drunk than I have ever seen anyone.

'They brought him home on two poles. He never stopped laughing all the way back, gesticulating with his arms and legs.

'This explained the mystery. My men also drank the juice of the grapes, and when they were so intoxicated they could not stir they went to sleep in the vineyard. As for Timbuctoo, his love of the vineyard was beyond all belief and all bounds. He lived in it as did the thrushes, whom he hated with the jealous hate of a rival. He repeated incessantly: "The thrushes eat all the grapes, captain!"

'One evening I was sent for. Something had been seen on the plain coming in our direction. I had not brought my field-glass and I could not distinguish things clearly. It looked like a great serpent uncoiling itself—a convoy. How could I tell?

'I sent some men to meet this strange caravan, which presently made its triumphal entry. Timbuctoo and nine of his comrades were carrying on a sort of altar made of camp stools eight severed, grinning and bleeding heads. The African was dragging along a horse to whose tail another head was fastened, and six other animals followed, adorned in the same manner.

'This is what I learned: Having started out to the vineyard, my Africans had suddenly perceived a detachment of Prussians approaching a village. Instead of taking to their heels, they hid themselves, and as soon as the Prussian officers dismounted at an inn to refresh themselves, the eleven rascals rushed on them, put to flight the lancers, who thought they were being attacked by the main army, killed the two sentries, then the colonel and the five officers of his escort.

'That day I kissed Timbuctoo. I saw, however, that he walked with difficulty and thought he was wounded. He laughed and said:

"Me provisions for my country."

'Timbuctoo was not fighting for glory, but for gain. Everything he found that seemed to him to be of the slightest value, especially anything that glistened, he put in his pocket. What a pocket! An abyss that began at his hips and reached to his ankles. He had retained an old term used by the troopers and called it his "profonde," and it was his "profonde" in fact.

'He had taken the gold lace off the Prussian uniforms, the brass off their helmets, detached their buttons, etc., and had thrown them all into his "profonde," which was full to overflowing.

'Each day he pocketed every glistening object that came beneath his observation, pieces of tin or pieces of silver, and sometimes his contour was very comical.

'He intended to carry all that back to the land of ostriches, whose brother he might have been, this son of a king, tormented with the longing to gobble up all objects that glistened. If he had not had his 'profonde' what would he have done? He doubtless would have swallowed them.

'Each morning his pocket was empty. He had, then, some general store where his riches were piled up. But where? I could not discover it.

'The general, on being informed of Timbuctoo's mighty act of valor, had the headless bodies that had been left in the neighboring village interred at once, that it might not be discovered that they were decapitated. The Prussians returned thither the following day. The mayor and seven prominent inhabitants were shot on the spot, by way of reprisal, as having denounced the Prussians.

'Winter was here. We were exhausted and desperate. There were skirmishes now every day. The famished men could no longer march. The eight 'Turcos' alone (three had been killed) remained fat and shiny, vigorous and always ready to fight. Timbuctoo was even getting fatter. He said to me one day:

"You much hungry; me good meat."

'And he brought me an excellent filet. But of what? We had no more cattle, nor sheep, nor goats, nor donkeys, nor pigs. It was impossible to get a horse. I thought of all this after I had devoured my meat. Then a horrible idea came to me. These negroes were born close to a country where they eat human beings! And each day such a number of soldiers were killed around the town! I questioned Timbuctoo. He would not answer. I did not insist, but from that time on, I declined his presents.

'He worshipped me. One night snow took us by surprise at the outposts. We were seated, on the ground. I looked with pity at those poor negroes shivering beneath this white frozen shower. I was very cold and began to cough. At once, I felt something fall on me like a large warm quilt. It was Timbuctoo's cape that he had thrown on my shoulders.

'I rose and returned his garment, saying:

"Keep it, my boy; you need it more than I do."

"Non, my lieutenant, for you; me no need. Me hot, hot!"

'And he looked at me entreatingly.

"Come, obey orders. Keep your cape; I insist," I replied.

'He then stood up, drew his sword, which he had sharpened to an edge like a scythe, and holding in his other hand the large cape which I had refused, said:

"If you not keep cape, me cut. No one cape."

'And he would have done it. So I yielded.

'Eight days later we capitulated. Some of us had been able to escape, the rest were to march out of the town and give themselves up to the conquerors.

'I went towards the exercising ground, where we were all to meet, when I was dumfounded at the sight of a gigantic negro dressed in white duck and wearing a straw hat. It was Timbuctoo. He was beaming and was walking with his hands in his pockets in front of a little shop where two plates and two glasses were displayed.

"What are you doing?" I said.

"Me not go. Me good cook; me make food for Colonel Algeria. Me eat Prussians; much steal, much."

'There were ten degrees of frost. I shivered at sight of this negro in white duck. He took me by the arm and made me go inside. I noticed an immense flag that he was going to place outside his door as soon as we had left, for he had some shame.

I read this sign, traced by the hand of some accomplice

"ARMY KITCHEN OF M. TIMBUCTOO,

"Formerly Cook to H. M. the Emperor.

"A Parisian Artist. Moderate Prices."

'In spite of the despair that was gnawing at my heart, I could not help laughing, and I left my negro to his new enterprise.

'Was not that better than taking him prisoner?

'You have just seen that he made a success of it, the rascal.

'Bezieres today belongs to the Germans. The "Restaurant Timbuctoo" is the beginning of a retaliation.'

13

TWO LITTLE SOLDIERS

Every Sunday, as soon as they were free, the little soldiers would go for a walk. They turned to the right on leaving the barracks, crossed Courbevoie with rapid strides, as though on a forced march; then, as the houses grew scarcer, they slowed down and followed the dusty road which leads to Bezons.

They were small and thin, lost in their ill-fitting capes, too large and too long, whose sleeves covered their hands; their ample red trousers fell in folds around their ankles. Under the high, stiff shako one could just barely perceive two thin, hollow-cheeked Breton faces, with their calm, naïve blue eyes. They never spoke during their journey, going straight before them, the same idea in each one's mind taking the place of conversation. For, at the entrance of the little forest of Champioux, they had found a spot which reminded them of home, and they did not feel happy anywhere else.

At the crossing of the Colombes and Chatou roads, when they arrived under the trees, they would take off their heavy, oppressive headgear and wipe their foreheads.

They always stopped for a while on the bridge at Bezons, and looked at the Seine. They stood there several minutes, bending over the railing, watching the white sails, which perhaps reminded them of their home, and of the fishing smacks leaving for the open.

As soon as they had crossed the Seine, they would purchase provisions at the delicatessen, the baker's, and the wine merchant's. A piece of bologna, four cents' worth of bread, and a quart of wine, made up the luncheon which they carried away, wrapped up in their handkerchiefs. But as soon as they were out of the village their gait would slacken and they would begin to talk.

Before them was a plain with a few clumps of trees, which led to the woods, a little forest which seemed to remind them of that other forest at Kermarivan. The wheat and oat fields bordered on the narrow path, and Jean Kerderen said each time to Luc Le Ganidec:

'It's just like home, just like Plounivon.'

'Yes, it's just like home.'

And they went on, side by side, their minds full of dim memories of home. They saw the fields, the hedges, the forests, and beaches.

Each time they stopped near a large stone on the edge of the private estate, because it reminded them of the dolmen of Locneuven.

As soon as they reached the first clump of trees, Luc Le Ganidec would cut off a small stick, and, whittling it slowly, would walk on, thinking of the folks at home.

Jean Kerderen carried the provisions.

From time to time Luc would mention a name, or allude to some boyish prank which would give them food for plenty of thought. And the home country, so dear and so distant, would little by little gain possession of their minds, sending them back through space, to the well-known forms and noises, to the familiar scenery, with the fragrance of its green fields and sea air. They no longer noticed the smells of the city. And in their dreams they saw their friends leaving, perhaps forever, for the dangerous fishing grounds.

They were walking slowly, Luc Le Ganidec and Jean Kerderen,

contented and sad, haunted by a sweet sorrow, the slow and penetrating sorrow of a captive animal which remembers the days of its freedom.

And when Luc had finished whittling his stick, they came to a little nook, where every Sunday they took their meal. They found the two bricks, which they had hidden in a hedge, and they made a little fire of dry branches and roasted their sausages on the ends of their knives.

When their last crumb of bread had been eaten and the last drop of wine had been drunk, they stretched themselves out on the grass side by side, without speaking, their half-closed eyes looking away in the distance, their hands clasped as in prayer, their red-trousered legs mingling with the bright colors of the wild flowers.

Towards noon they glanced, from time to time, towards the village of Bezons, for the dairy maid would soon be coming. Every Sunday she would pass in front of them on the way to milk her cow, the only cow in the neighborhood which was sent out to pasture.

Soon they would see the girl, coming through the fields, and it pleased them to watch the sparkling sunbeams reflected from her shining pail. They never spoke of her. They were just glad to see her, without understanding why.

She was a tall, strapping girl, freckled and tanned by the open air—a girl typical of the Parisian suburbs.

Once, on noticing that they were always sitting in the same place, she said to them:

'Do you always come here?'

Luc Le Ganidec, more daring than his friend, stammered:

'Yes, we come here for our rest.'

That was all. But the following Sunday, on seeing them, she smiled with the kindly smile of a woman who understood their shyness, and she asked:

'What are you doing here? Are you watching the grass grow?'

Luc, cheered up, smiled: 'P'raps.'

She continued: 'It's not growing fast, is it?'

He answered, still laughing: 'Not exactly.'

She went on. But when she came back with her pail full of milk, she stopped before them and said:

'Want some? It will remind you of home.'

She had, perhaps instinctively, guessed and touched the right spot.

Both were moved. Then not without difficulty, she poured some milk into the bottle in which they had brought their wine. Luc started to drink, carefully watching lest he should take more than his share. Then he passed the bottle to Jean. She stood before them, her hands on her hips, her pail at her feet, enjoying the pleasure that she was giving them. Then she went on, saying: 'Well, bye-bye until next Sunday!'

For a long time they watched her tall form as it receded in the distance, blending with the background, and finally disappeared.

The following week as they left the barracks, Jean said to Luc:

'Don't you think we ought to buy her something good?'

They were sorely perplexed by the problem of choosing something to bring to the dairy maid. Luc was in favor of bringing her some chitterlings; but Jean, who had a sweet tooth, thought that candy would be the best thing. He won, and so they went to a grocery to buy two sous' worth, of red and white candies.

This time they ate more quickly than usual, excited by anticipation.

Jean was the first one to notice her. 'There she is,' he said; and Luc answered: 'Yes, there she is.'

She smiled when she saw them, and cried:

'Well, how are you today?'

They both answered together:

'All right! How's everything with you?'

Then she started to talk of simple things which might interest them; of the weather, of the crops, of her masters.

They didn't dare to offer their candies, which were slowly melting in Jean's pocket. Finally Luc, growing bolder, murmured:

'We have brought you something.'

She asked: 'Let's see it.'

Then Jean, blushing to the tips of his ears, reached in his pocket, and drawing out the little paper bag, handed it to her.

She began to eat the little sweet dainties. The two soldiers sat in front of her, moved and delighted.

At last she went to do her milking, and when she came back she again gave them some milk.

They thought of her all through the week and often spoke of her: The following Sunday she sat beside them for a longer time.

The three of them sat there, side by side, their eyes looking far away in the distance, their hands clasped over their knees, and they told each other little incidents and little details of the villages where they were born, while the cow, waiting to be milked, stretched her heavy head toward the girl and mooed.

Soon the girl consented to eat with them and to take a sip of wine. Often she brought them plums pocket for plums were now ripe. Her presence enlivened the little Breton soldiers, who chattered away like two birds.

One Tuesday, something unusual happened to Luc Le Ganidec; he asked for leave and did not return until ten o'clock at night.

Jean, worried and racked his brain to account for his friend's having obtained leave.

The following Friday, Luc borrowed ten sons from one of his friends, and once more asked and obtained leave for several hours.

When he started out with Jean on Sunday he seemed queer, disturbed, changed. Kerderen did not understand; he vaguely suspected something, but he could not guess what it might be.

They went straight to the usual place, and lunched slowly. Neither was hungry.

Soon the girl appeared. They watched her approach as they always did. When she was near, Luc arose and went towards her. She placed her pail on the ground and kissed him. She kissed him passionately, throwing her arms around his neck, without paying attention to Jean, without even noticing that he was there.

Poor Jean was dazed, so dazed that he could not understand. His mind was upset and his heart broken, without his even realizing why.

Then the girl sat down beside Luc, and they started to chat.

Jean was not looking at them. He understood now why his friend had gone out twice during the week. He felt the pain and the sting which treachery and deceit leave in their wake.

Luc and the girl went together to attend to the cow.

Jean followed them with his eyes. He saw them disappear side by side, the red trousers of his friend making a scarlet spot against the white road. It was Luc who sank the stake to which the cow was tethered. The girl stooped down to milk the cow, while he absent-mindedly stroked the animal's glossy neck. Then they left the pail in the grass and disappeared in the woods.

Jean could no longer see anything but the wall of leaves through which they had passed. He was unmanned so that he did not have strength to stand. He stayed there, motionless, bewildered and grieving—simple, passionate grief. He wanted to weep, to run away, to hide somewhere, never to see anyone again.

Then he saw them coming back again. They were walking slowly, hand in hand, as village lovers do. Luc was carrying the pail.

After kissing him again, the girl went on, nodding carelessly to Jean. She did not offer him any milk that day.

The two little soldiers sat side by side, motionless as always, silent and quiet, their calm faces in no way betraying the trouble in their hearts. The sun shone down on them. From time to time, they could hear the plaintive lowing of the cow. At the usual time they arose to return.

Luc was whittling a stick. Jean carried the empty bottle. He left it at the wine merchant's in Bezons. Then they stopped on the bridge, as they did every Sunday, and watched the water flowing by.

Jean leaned over the railing, farther and farther, as though he had seen something in the stream which hypnotized him. Luc said to him:

'What's the matter? Do you want a drink?'

He had hardly said the last word when Jean's head carried away the rest of his body, and the little blue and red soldier fell like a shot and disappeared in the water.

Luc, paralyzed with horror, tried vainly to shout for help. In the distance he saw something move; then his friend's head bobbed up out of the water only to disappear again.

Farther down he again noticed a hand, just one hand, which appeared and again went out of sight. That was all.

The boatmen who had rushed to the scene found the body that day.

Luc ran back to the barracks, crazed, and with eyes and voice full of tears, he related the accident: 'He leaned—he—he was leaning—so far over—that his head carried him away—and—he—fell—he fell—'

Emotion choked him so that he could say no more. If he had only known.

14

THE COLONEL'S IDEAS

'Upon my word,' said Colonel Laporte, 'although I am old and gouty, my legs as stiff as two pieces of wood, yet if a pretty woman were to tell me to go through the eye of a needle, I believe I should take a jump at it, like a clown through a hoop. I shall die like that; it is in the blood. I am an old beau, one of the old school, and the sight of a woman, a pretty woman, stirs me to the tips of my toes. There!

'We are all very much alike in France in this respect; we still remain knights, knights of love and fortune, since God has been abolished whose bodyguard we really were. But nobody can ever get woman out of our hearts; there she is, and there she will remain, and we love her, and shall continue to love her, and go on committing all kinds of follies on her account as long as there is a France on the map of Europe; and even if France were to be wiped off the map, there would always be Frenchmen left.

'When I am in the presence of a woman, of a pretty woman, I feel capable of anything. By Jove! When I feel her looks penetrating me, her confounded looks which set your blood on fire, I should like to do I don't know what; to fight a duel, to have a row, to smash the furniture, in order to show that I am the strongest, the bravest, the most daring and the most devoted of men.

'But I am not the only one, certainly not; the whole French

army is like me, I swear to you. From the common soldier to the general, we all start out, from the van to the rear guard, when there is a woman in the case, a pretty woman. Do you remember what Joan of Arc made us do formerly? Come. I will make a bet that if a pretty woman had taken command of the army on the eve of Sedan, when Marshal MacMahon was wounded, we should have broken through the Prussian lines, by Jove! And had a drink out of their guns.

'It was not a Trochu, but a Sainte-Genevieve, who was needed in Paris; and I remember a little anecdote of the war which proves that we are capable of everything in presence of a woman.

'I was a captain, a simple captain, at the time, and I was in command of a detachment of scouts, who were retreating through a district which swarmed with Prussians. We were surrounded, pursued, tired out and half dead with fatigue and hunger, but we were bound to reach Bar-sur-Tain before the morrow, otherwise we should be shot, cut down, massacred. I do not know how we managed to escape so far. However, we had ten leagues to go during the night, ten leagues through the night, ten leagues through the snow, and with empty stomachs, and I thought to myself:

'It is all over; my poor devils of fellows will never be able to do it.'

'We had eaten nothing since the day before, and the whole day long we remained hidden in a barn, huddled close together, so as not to feel the cold so much, unable to speak or even move, and sleeping by fits and starts, as one does when worn out with fatigue.

'It was dark by five o'clock, that wan darkness of the snow, and I shook my men. Some of them would not get up; they were almost incapable of moving or of standing upright; their joints were stiff from cold and hunger.

'Before us there was a large expanse of flat, bare country; the snow was still falling like a curtain, in large, white flakes, which concealed everything under a thick, frozen coverlet, a coverlet of frozen wool. One might have thought that it was the end of the world.

"Come, my lads, let us start."

'They looked at the thick white flakes that were coming down, and they seemed to think: "We have had enough of this; we may just as well die here!" Then I took out my revolver and said:

"I will shoot the first man who flinches." And so they set off, but very slowly, like men whose legs were of very little use to them, and I sent four of them three hundred yards ahead to scout, and the others followed pell-mell, walking at random and without any order. I put the strongest in the rear, with orders to quicken the pace of the sluggards with the points of their bayonets in the back.

'The snow seemed as if it were going to bury us alive; it powdered our kepis and cloaks without melting, and made phantoms of us, a kind of spectres of dead, weary soldiers. I said to myself: "We shall never get out of this except by a miracle."

'Sometimes we had to stop for a few minutes, on account of those who could not follow us, and then we heard nothing except the falling snow, that vague, almost undiscernible sound made by the falling flakes. Some of the men shook themselves, others did not move, and so I gave the order to set off again. They shouldered their rifles, and with weary feet we resumed our march, when suddenly the scouts fell back. Something had alarmed them; they had heard voices in front of them. I sent forward six men and a sergeant and waited.

'All at once a shrill cry, a woman's cry, pierced through the heavy silence of the snow, and in a few minutes they brought back two prisoners, an old man and a girl, whom I questioned in a low voice. They were escaping from the Prussians, who had occupied their house during the evening and had got drunk. The father was alarmed on his daughter's account, and, without even telling their servants, they had made their escape in the darkness.

I saw immediately that they belonged to the better class. I invited them to accompany us, and we started off again, the old man who knew the road acting as our guide.

'It had ceased snowing, the stars appeared and the cold became intense. The girl, who was leaning on her father's arm, walked unsteadily as though in pain, and several times she murmured:

"I have no feeling at all in my feet"; and I suffered more than she did to see that poor little woman dragging herself like that through the snow. But suddenly she stopped and said:

"Father, I am so tired that I cannot go any further."

'The old man wanted to carry her, but he could not even lift her up, and she sank to the ground with a deep sigh. We all gathered round her, and, as for me, I stamped my foot in perplexity, not knowing what to do, and being unwilling to abandon that man and girl like that, when suddenly one of the soldiers, a Parisian whom they had nicknamed Pratique, said:

"Come, comrades, we must carry the young lady, otherwise we shall not show ourselves Frenchmen, confound it!"

'I really believe that I swore with pleasure. "That is very good of you, my children," I said; "and I will take my share of the burden."

'We could indistinctly see, through the darkness, the trees of a little wood on the left. Several of the men went into it, and soon came back with a bundle of branches made into a litter.

"Who will lend his cape? It is for a pretty girl, comrades," Pratique said, and ten cloaks were thrown to him. In a moment the girl was lying, warm and comfortable, among them, and was raised upon six shoulders. I placed myself at their head, on the right, well pleased with my position.

'We started off much more briskly, as if we had had a drink of wine, and I even heard some jokes. A woman is quite enough to electrify Frenchmen, you see. The soldiers, who had become cheerful and warm, had almost reformed their ranks, and an old "franc-tireur" who was following the litter, waiting for his turn to replace the first of his comrades who might give out, said to one of his neighbors, loud enough for me to hear: "I am not a young man now, but by——, there is nothing like the women to put courage into you!"

'We went on, almost without stopping, until three o'clock in the morning, when suddenly our scouts fell back once more, and soon the whole detachment showed nothing but a vague shadow on the ground, as the men lay on the snow. I gave my orders in a low voice, and heard the harsh, metallic sound of the cocking, of rifles. For there, in the middle of the plain, some strange object was moving about. It looked like some enormous animal running about, now stretching out like a serpent, now coiling itself into a ball, darting to the right, then to the left, then stopping, and presently starting off again. But, presently, that wandering shape came nearer, and I saw a dozen lancers at full gallop, one behind the other. They had lost their way and were trying to find it.

'They were so near by that time that I could hear the loud breathing of their horses, the clinking of their swords and the creaking of their saddles, and cried: "Fire!"

'Fifty rifle shots broke the stillness of the night, then there were four or five reports, and at last one single shot was heard, and when the smoke had cleared away, we saw that the twelve men and nine horses had fallen. Three of the animals were galloping away at a furious pace, and one of them was dragging the dead body of its rider, which rebounded violently from the ground; his foot had caught in the stirrup.

'One of the soldiers behind me gave a terrible laugh and said: "There will be some widows there!"

'Perhaps he was married. A third added: "It did not take long!"

'A head emerged from the litter.

"What is the matter?" she asked; "are you fighting?"

"It is nothing, mademoiselle," I replied; "we have got rid of a dozen Prussians!"

"Poor fellows!" she said. But as she was cold, she quickly disappeared beneath the cloaks again, and we started off once more. We marched on for a long time, and at last the sky began to grow lighter. The snow became quite clear, luminous and glistening, and a rosy tint appeared in the east. Suddenly a voice in the distance cried:

"Who goes there?"

'The whole detachment halted, and I advanced to give the countersign. We had reached the French lines, and, as my men defiled before the outpost, a commandant on horseback, whom I had informed of what had taken place, asked in a sonorous voice, as he saw the litter pass him: "What have you in there?"

'And immediately a small head covered with light hair appeared, dishevelled and smiling, and replied:

"It is I, monsieur."

'At this, the men raised a hearty laugh, and we felt quite light-hearted, while Pratique, who was walking by the side of the litter, waved his kepi and shouted:

"Vive la France!" And I felt really affected. I do not know why, except that I thought it a pretty and gallant thing to say.

'It seemed to me as if we had just saved the whole of France and had done something that other men could not have done, something simple and really patriotic. I shall never forget that little face, you may be sure; and if I had to give my opinion about abolishing drums, trumpets and bugles, I should propose to replace them in every regiment by a pretty girl, and that would be even better than playing the "Marseillaise." By Jove! it would put some spirit into a trooper to have a Madonna like that, a live Madonna, by the colonel's side.'

He was silent for a few moments and then continued, with an air of conviction, and nodding his head:

'All the same, we are very fond of women, we Frenchmen!'

15

MOTHER SAUVAGE

Fifteen years had passed since I was at Virelogne. I returned there in the autumn to shoot with my friend Serval, who had at last rebuilt his chateau, which the Prussians had destroyed.

I loved that district. It is one of those delightful spots which have a sensuous charm for the eyes. You love it with a physical love. We, whom the country enchants, keep tender memories of certain springs, certain woods, certain pools, certain hills seen very often which have stirred us like joyful events. Sometimes our thoughts turn back to a corner in a forest, or the end of a bank, or orchard filled with flowers, seen but a single time on some bright day, yet remaining in our hearts like the image of certain women met in the street on a spring morning in their light, gauzy dresses, leaving in soul and body an unsatisfied desire which is not to be forgotten, a feeling that you have just passed by happiness.

At Virelogne, I loved the whole countryside, dotted with little woods and crossed by brooks which sparkled in the sun and looked like veins carrying blood to the earth. You fished in them for crawfish, trout and eels. Divine happiness! You could bathe in places and you often found snipe among the high grass which grew along the borders of these small water courses.

I was stepping along light as a goat, watching my two dogs running ahead of me; Serval, a hundred metres to my right, was beating a field of lucerne. I turned round by the thicket which forms the boundary of the wood of Sandres and I saw a cottage in ruins.

Suddenly I remembered it as I had seen it the last time, in 1869, neat, covered with vines, with chickens before the door. What is sadder than a dead house, with its skeleton standing bare and sinister?

I also recalled that inside its doors, after a very tiring day, the good woman had given me a glass of wine to drink and that Serval had told me the history of its people. The father, an old poacher, had been killed by the gendarmes. The son, whom I had once seen, was a tall, dry fellow who also passed for a fierce slayer of game. People called them 'Les Sauvage.'

Was that a name or a nickname?

I called to Serval. He came up with his long strides like a crane.

I asked him: 'What's become of those people?'

This was his story: when war was declared the son Sauvage, who was then thirty-three years old, enlisted, leaving his mother alone in the house. People did not pity the old woman very much because she had money; they knew it.

She remained entirely alone in that isolated dwelling, so far from the village, on the edge of the wood. She was not afraid, however, being of the same strain as the men folk—a hardy old woman, tall and thin, who seldom laughed and with whom one never jested. The women of the fields laugh but little in any case, that is men's business. But they themselves have sad and narrowed hearts, leading a melancholy, gloomy life. The peasants imbibe a little noisy merriment at the tavern, but their helpmates always have grave, stern countenances. The muscles of their faces have never learned the motions of laughter.

Mother Sauvage continued her ordinary existence in her cottage, which was soon covered by the snows. She came to the village once a week to get bread and a little meat. Then she returned to her house. As there was talk of wolves, she went out with a gun upon her shoulder—her son's gun, rusty and with the butt worn by the rubbing of the hand—and she was a strange sight, the tall 'Sauvage,' a little bent, going with slow strides over the snow, the muzzle of the piece extending beyond the black headdress, which confined her head and imprisoned her white hair, which no one had ever seen.

One day a Prussian force arrived. It was billeted upon the inhabitants, according to the property and resources of each. Four were allotted to the old woman, who was known to be rich.

They were four great fellows with fair complexion, blond beards and blue eyes, who had not grown thin in spite of the fatigue which they had endured already and who also, though in a conquered country, had remained kind and gentle. Alone with this aged woman, they showed themselves full of consideration, sparing her, as much as they could, all expense and fatigue. They could be seen, all four of them, making their toilet at the well in their shirt-sleeves in the gray dawn, splashing with great swishes of water their pink-white northern skin, while La Mere Sauvage went and came, preparing their soup. They would be seen cleaning the kitchen, rubbing the tiles, splitting wood, peeling potatoes, doing up all the housework like four good sons around their mother.

But the old woman thought always of her own son, so tall and thin, with his hooked nose and his brown eyes and his heavy mustache which made a roll of black hair upon his lip. She asked every day of each of the soldiers who were installed beside her hearth: 'Do you know where the French marching regiment, No. 23, was sent? My boy is in it.'

They invariably answered, 'no, we don't know, don't know a thing at all.' And, understanding her pain and her uneasiness—they who had mothers, too, there at home—they rendered her a thousand little services. She loved them well, moreover, her four enemies, since the peasantry have no patriotic hatred; that belongs to the upper class alone. The humble, those who pay the most because they are poor and because every new burden crushes them down; those who are killed in masses, who make the true cannon's prey because they are so many; those, in fine, who suffer most cruelly the atrocious miseries of war because they are the feeblest and offer least resistance—they hardly understand at all those bellicose ardors, that excitable sense of honor or those pretended political combinations which in six months exhaust two nations, the conqueror with the conquered.

They said in the district, in speaking of the Germans of La Mere Sauvage:

'There are four who have found a soft place.'

Now, one morning, when the old woman was alone in the house, she observed, far off on the plain, a man coming toward her dwelling. Soon she recognized him; it was the postman to distribute the letters. He gave her a folded paper and she drew out of her case the spectacles which she used for sewing. Then she read:

MADAME SAUVAGE:

This letter is to tell you sad news. Your boy Victor was killed yesterday by a shell which almost cut him in two.

I was near by, as we stood next each other in the company, and he told me about you and asked me to let you know on the same day if anything happened to him.

I took his watch, which was in his pocket, to bring it back to you when the war is done.

CESAIRE RIVOT,

Soldier of the 2d class, March. Reg. No. 23.

The letter was dated three weeks back.

She did not cry at all. She remained motionless, so overcome and stupefied that she did not even suffer as yet. She thought: 'There's Victor killed now.' Then little by little the tears came to her eyes and the sorrow filled her heart. Her thoughts came, one by one, dreadful, torturing. She would never kiss him again, her child, her big boy, never again! The gendarmes had killed the father, the Prussians had killed the son. He had been cut in two by a cannon-ball. She seemed to see the thing, the horrible thing: the head falling, the eyes open, while he chewed the corner of his big mustache as he always did in moments of anger.

What had they done with his body afterward? If they had only let her have her boy back as they had brought back her husband—with the bullet in the middle of the forehead!

But she heard a noise of voices. It was the Prussians returning from the village. She hid her letter very quickly in her pocket, and she received them quietly, with her ordinary face, having had time to wipe her eyes.

They were laughing, all four, delighted, for they brought with them a fine rabbit—stolen, doubtless—and they made signs to the old woman that there was to be something good to eat.

She set herself to work at once to prepare breakfast, but when it came to killing the rabbit, her heart failed her. And yet it was not the first. One of the soldiers struck it down with a blow of his fist behind the ears.

The beast once dead, she skinned the red body, but the sight of the blood which she was touching, and which covered her hands, and which she felt cooling and coagulating, made her tremble from head to foot, and she kept seeing her big boy cut in two, bloody, like this still palpitating animal.

She sat down at table with the Prussians, but she could not eat, not even a mouthful. They devoured the rabbit without bothering themselves about her. She looked at them sideways, without speaking, her face so impassive that they perceived nothing.

All of a sudden she said: 'I don't even know your names, and here's a whole month that we've been together.' They understood, not without difficulty, what she wanted, and told their names.

That was not sufficient; she had them written for her on a paper, with the addresses of their families, and, resting her spectacles on her great nose, she contemplated that strange handwriting, then folded the sheet and put it in her pocket, on top of the letter which told her of the death of her son.

When the meal was ended she said to the men:

'I am going to work for you.'

And she began to carry up hay into the loft where they slept.

They were astonished at her taking all this trouble; she explained to them that thus they would not be so cold; and they helped her. They heaped the stacks of hay as high as the straw roof, and in that manner they made a sort of great chamber with four walls of fodder, warm and perfumed, where they should sleep splendidly.

At dinner, one of them was worried to see that La Mere Sauvage still ate nothing. She told him that she had pains in her stomach. Then she kindled a good fire to warm herself, and the four Germans ascended to their lodging-place by the ladder which served them every night for this purpose.

As soon as they closed the trapdoor, the old woman removed the ladder, then opened the outside door noiselessly and went back to look for more bundles of straw, with which she filled her kitchen. She went barefoot in the snow, so softly that no sound was heard. From time to time she listened to the sonorous and unequal snoring of the four soldiers who were fast asleep.

When she judged her preparations to be sufficient, she threw one of the bundles into the fireplace, and when it was alight she scattered it over all the others. Then she went outside again and looked.

In a few seconds, the whole interior of the cottage was illumined with a brilliant light and became a frightful brasier, a gigantic fiery furnace, whose glare streamed out of the narrow window and threw a glittering beam upon the snow.

Then a great cry issued from the top of the house; it was a clamor of men shouting heartrending calls of anguish and of terror. Finally the trapdoor having given way, a whirlwind of fire shot up into the loft, pierced the straw roof, rose to the sky like the immense flame of a torch, and all the cottage flared.

Nothing more was heard therein but the crackling of the fire, the cracking of the walls, the falling of the rafters. Suddenly the roof fell in and the burning carcass of the dwelling hurled a great plume of sparks into the air, amid a cloud of smoke.

The country, all white, lit up by the fire, shone like a cloth of silver tinted with red.

A bell, far off, began to toll.

The old 'Sauvage' stood before her ruined dwelling, armed with her gun, her son's gun, for fear one of those men might escape.

When she saw that it was ended, she threw her weapon into the brasier. A loud report followed.

People were coming, the peasants, the Prussians.

They found the woman seated on the trunk of a tree, calm and satisfied.

A German officer, but speaking French like a son of France, demanded:

'Where are your soldiers?'

She reached her bony arm toward the red heap of fire which was almost out and answered with a strong voice:

'There!'

They crowded round her. The Prussian asked:

'How did it take fire?'

'It was I who set it on fire.'

They did not believe her, they thought that the sudden disaster had made her crazy. While all pressed round and listened, she told the story from beginning to end, from the arrival of the letter to the last shriek of the men who were burned with her house, and never omitted a detail.

When she had finished, she drew two pieces of paper from her pocket, and, in order to distinguish them by the last gleams of the fire, she again adjusted her spectacles. Then she said, showing one: 'That, that is the death of Victor.' Showing the other, she added, indicating the red ruins with a bend of the head: 'Here are their names, so that you can write home.' She quietly held a sheet of paper out to the officer, who held her by the shoulders, and she continued:

'You must write how it happened, and you must say to their mothers that it was I who did that, Victoire Simon, la Sauvage! Do not forget.'

The officer shouted some orders in German. They seized her, they threw her against the walls of her house, still hot. Then twelve men drew quickly up before her, at twenty paces. She did not move. She had understood; she waited.

An order rang out, followed instantly by a long report. A belated shot went off by itself, after the others.

The old woman did not fall. She sank as though they had cut off her legs.

The Prussian officer approached. She was almost cut in two, and in her withered hand she held her letter bathed with blood.

My friend Serval added:

'It was by way of reprisal that the Germans destroyed the chateau of the district, which belonged to me.'

I thought of the mothers of those four fine fellows burned in that house and of the horrible heroism of that other mother shot against the wall.

And I picked up a little stone, still blackened by the flames.

16

USELESS BEAUTY

About half-past five one afternoon at the end of June when the sun was shining warm and bright into the large courtyard, a very elegant victoria with two beautiful black horses drew up in front of the mansion.

The Comtesse de Mascaret came down the steps just as her husband, who was coming home, appeared in the carriage entrance. He stopped for a few moments to look at his wife and turned rather pale. The countess was very beautiful, graceful and distinguished looking, with her long oval face, her complexion like yellow ivory, her large gray eyes and her black hair; and she got into her carriage without looking at him, without even seeming to have noticed him, with such a particularly high-bred air, that the furious jealousy by which he had been devoured for so long again gnawed at his heart. He went up to her and said: 'You are going for a drive?'

She merely replied disdainfully: 'You see I am!'

'In the Bois de Boulogne?'

'Most probably.'

'May I come with you?'

'The carriage belongs to you.'

Without being surprised at the tone in which she answered him, he got in and sat down by his wife's side and said: 'Bois de

Boulogne.' The footman jumped up beside the coachman, and the horses as usual pranced and tossed their heads until they were in the street. Husband and wife sat side by side without speaking. He was thinking how to begin a conversation, but she maintained such an obstinately hard look that he did not venture to make the attempt. At last, however, he cunningly, accidentally as it were, touched the countess' gloved hand with his own, but she drew her arm away with a movement which was so expressive of disgust that he remained thoughtful, in spite of his usual authoritative and despotic character, and he said: 'Gabrielle!'

'What do you want?'

'I think you are looking adorable.'

She did not reply, but remained lying back in the carriage, looking like an irritated queen. By that time they were driving up the Champs Elysees, toward the Arc de Triomphe. That immense monument, at the end of the long avenue, raised its colossal arch against the red sky and the sun seemed to be descending on it, showering fiery dust on it from the sky.

The stream of carriages, with dashes of sunlight reflected in the silver trappings of the harness and the glass of the lamps, flowed on in a double current toward the town and toward the Bois, and the Comte de Mascaret continued: 'My dear Gabrielle!'

Unable to control herself any longer, she replied in an exasperated voice: 'Oh! Do leave me in peace, pray! I am not even allowed to have my carriage to myself now.' He pretended not to hear her and continued: 'You never have looked so pretty as you do today.'

Her patience had come to an end, and she replied with irrepressible anger: 'You are wrong to notice it, for I swear to you that I will never have anything to do with you in that way again.'

The count was decidedly stupefied and upset, and, his violent nature gaining the upper hand, he exclaimed: 'What do you mean by that?' in a tone that betrayed rather the brutal master than the lover. She replied in a low voice, so that the servants might not hear amid the deafening noise of the wheels: 'Ah! What do I mean by that? What do I mean by that? Now I recognize you again! Do you want me to tell everything?'

'Yes.'

'Everything that has weighed on my heart since I have been the victim of your terrible selfishness?'

He had grown red with surprise and anger and he growled between his closed teeth: 'Yes, tell me everything.'

He was a tall, broad-shouldered man, with a big red beard, a handsome man, a nobleman, a man of the world, who passed as a perfect husband and an excellent father, and now, for the first time since they had started, she turned toward him and looked him full in the face: 'Ah! You will hear some disagreeable things, but you must know that I am prepared for everything, that I fear nothing, and you less than any one today.'

He also was looking into her eyes and was already shaking with rage, as he said in a low voice: 'You are mad.'

'No, but I will no longer be the victim of the hateful penalty of maternity, which you have inflicted on me for eleven years! I wish to take my place in society as I have the right to do, as all women have the right to do.'

He suddenly grew pale again and stammered: 'I do not understand you.'

'Oh! yes; you understand me well enough. It is now three months since I had my last child, and as I am still very beautiful, and as, in spite of all your efforts you cannot spoil my figure, as you just now perceived, when you saw me on the doorstep, you think it is time that I should think of having another child.'

'But you are talking nonsense!'

'No, I am not, I am thirty, and I have had seven children, and we have been married eleven years, and you hope that this will go on for ten years longer, after which you will leave off being jealous.'

He seized her arm and squeezed it, saying: 'I will not allow you to talk to me like that much longer.'

'And I shall talk to you till the end, until I have finished all I have to say to you, and if you try to prevent me, I shall raise my voice so that the two servants, who are on the box, may hear. I only allowed you to come with me for that object, for I have these witnesses who will oblige you to listen to me and to contain yourself, so now pay attention to what I say. I have always felt an antipathy to you, and I have always let you see it, for I have never lied, monsieur. You married me in spite of myself; you forced my parents, who were in embarrassed circumstances, to give me to you, because you were rich, and they obliged me to marry you in spite of my tears.

'So you bought me, and as soon as I was in your power, as soon as I had become your companion, ready to attach myself to you, to forget your coercive and threatening proceedings, in order that I might only remember that I ought to be a devoted wife and to love you as much as it might be possible for me to love you, you became jealous, you, as no man has ever been before, with the base, ignoble jealousy of a spy, which was as degrading to you as it was to me. I had not been married eight months when you suspected me of every perfidiousness, and you even told me so. What a disgrace! And as you could not prevent me from being beautiful and from pleasing people, from being called in drawing-rooms and also in the newspapers one of the most beautiful women in Paris, you tried everything you could think of to keep admirers from me, and you hit upon the abominable idea of making me spend my life in a constant state of motherhood, until the time should come when I should disgust every man. Oh, do not deny it. I did not understand it for some time, but then I guessed it. You even boasted about it to your sister, who told me of it, for she is fond of me and was disgusted at your boorish coarseness.

'Ah! Remember how you have behaved in the past! How for eleven years you have compelled me to give up all society and simply be a mother to your children. And then you would grow disgusted with me and I was sent into the country, the family chateau, among fields and meadows. And when I reappeared, fresh, pretty and unspoiled, still seductive and constantly surrounded by admirers, hoping that at last I should live a little more like a rich young society woman, you were seized with jealousy again, and you began once more to persecute me with that infamous and hateful desire from which you are suffering at this moment by my side. And it is not the desire of possessing me—for I should never have refused myself to you, but it is the wish to make me unsightly.

'And then that abominable and mysterious thing occurred which I was a long time in understanding (but I grew sharp by dint of watching your thoughts and actions): you attached yourself to your children with all the security which they gave you while I bore them. You felt affection for them, with all your aversion to me, and in spite of your ignoble fears, which were momentarily allayed by your pleasure in seeing me lose my symmetry.

'Oh! How often have I noticed that joy in you! I have seen it in your eyes and guessed it. You loved your children as victories, and not because they were of your own blood. They were victories over me, over my youth, over my beauty, over my charms, over the compliments which were paid me and over those that were whispered around me without being paid to me personally. And you are proud of them, you make a parade of them, you take them out for drives in your break in the Bois de Boulogne and you give them donkey rides at Montmorency. You take them to theatrical matinees so that you may be seen in the midst of them, so that the people may say: "What a kind father" and that it may be repeated—'

He had seized her wrist with savage brutality, and he squeezed it so violently that she was quiet and nearly cried out with the pain and he said to her in a whisper:

'I love my children, do you hear? What you have just told me is disgraceful in a mother. But you belong to me; I am master—your master—I can exact from you what I like and when I like—and I have the law-on my side.'

He was trying to crush her fingers in the strong grip of his large, muscular hand, and she, livid with pain, tried in vain to free them from that vise which was crushing them. The agony made her breathe hard and the tears came into her eyes. 'You see that I am the master and the stronger,' he said. When he somewhat loosened his grip, she asked him: 'Do you think that I am a religious woman?'

He was surprised and stammered 'Yes.'

'Do you think that I could lie if I swore to the truth of anything to you before an altar on which Christ's body is?'

'No.'

'Will you go with me to some church?'

'What for?'

'You shall see. Will you?'

'If you absolutely wish it, yes.'

She raised her voice and said: 'Philippe!' And the coachman, bending down a little, without taking his eyes from his horses, seemed to turn his ear alone toward his mistress, who continued: 'Drive to St. Philippe-du-Roule.' And the victoria, which had reached the entrance of the Bois de Boulogne, returned to Paris.

Husband and wife did not exchange a word further during the drive, and when the carriage stopped before the church Madame de Mascaret jumped out and entered it, followed by the count, a few yards distant. She went, without stopping, as far as the choir-screen, and falling on her knees at a chair, she buried her face in her hands. She prayed for a long time, and he, standing behind her could see that she was crying. She wept noiselessly, as women weep when they are in great, poignant grief. There was a kind of undulation in her body, which ended in a little sob, which was hidden and stifled by her fingers.

But the Comte de Mascaret thought that the situation was lasting too long, and he touched her on the shoulder. That contact recalled her to herself, as if she had been burned, and getting up, she looked straight into his eyes. 'This is what I have to say to you. I am afraid of nothing, whatever you may do to me. You may kill me if you like. One of your children is not yours, and one only; that I swear to you before God, who hears me here. That was the only revenge that was possible for me in return for all your abominable masculine tyrannies, in return for the penal servitude of childbearing to which you have condemned me. Who was my lover? That you never will know! You may suspect every one, but you never will find out. I gave myself to him, without love and without pleasure, only for the sake of betraying you, and he also made me a mother. Which is the child? That also you never will know. I have seven; try to find out! I intended to tell you this later, for one has not avenged oneself on a man by deceiving him, unless he knows it. You have driven me to confess it today. I have now finished.'

She hurried through the church toward the open door, expecting to hear behind her the quick step: of her husband whom she had defied and to be knocked to the ground by a blow of his fist, but she heard nothing and reached her carriage. She jumped into it at a bound, overwhelmed with anguish and breathless with fear. So she called out to the coachman: 'Home!' and the horses set off at a quick trot.

The Comtesse de Mascaret was waiting in her room for dinner time as a criminal sentenced to death awaits the hour of his execution. What was her husband going to do? Had he come home? Despotic, passionate, ready for any violence as he was, what was he meditating, what had he made up his mind to do?

There was no sound in the house, and every moment she looked at the clock. Her lady's maid had come and dressed her for the evening and had then left the room again. Eight o'clock struck and almost at the same moment there were two knocks at the door, and the butler came in and announced dinner.

'Has the count come in?'

'Yes, Madame la Comtesse. He is in the dining room.'

For a little moment, she felt inclined to arm herself with a small revolver which she had bought some time before, foreseeing the tragedy which was being rehearsed in her heart. But she remembered that all the children would be there, and she took nothing except a bottle of smelling salts. He rose somewhat ceremoniously from his chair. They exchanged a slight bow and sat down. The three boys with their tutor, Abbe Martin, were on her right and the three girls, with Miss Smith, their English governess, were on her left. The youngest child, who was only three months old, remained upstairs with his nurse.

The abbe said grace as usual when there was no company, for the children did not come down to dinner when guests were present. Then they began dinner. The countess, suffering from emotion, which she had not calculated upon, remained with her eyes cast down, while the count scrutinized now the three boys and now the three girls. with an uncertain, unhappy expression, which travelled from one to the other. Suddenly pushing his wineglass from him, it broke, and the wine was spilt on the tablecloth, and at the slight noise caused by this little accident the countess started up from her chair; and for the first time they looked at each other. Then, in spite of themselves, in spite of the irritation of their nerves caused by every glance, they continued to exchange looks, rapid as pistol shots.

The abbe, who felt that there was some cause for embarrassment which he could not divine, attempted to begin a conversation and tried various subjects, but his useless efforts gave rise to no ideas and did not bring out a word. The countess, with feminine tact and obeying her instincts of a woman of the world, attempted to answer him two or three times, but in vain. She could not find words, in the perplexity of her mind, and her own voice almost frightened her in the silence of the large room, where nothing was heard except the slight sound of plates and knives and forks.

Suddenly her husband said to her, bending forward: 'Here, amid your children, will you swear to me that what you told me just now is true?'

The hatred which was fermenting in her veins suddenly roused her, and replying to that question with the same firmness with which she had replied to his looks, she raised both her hands, the right pointing toward the boys and the left toward the girls, and said in a firm, resolute voice and without any hesitation: 'On the head of my children, I swear that I have told you the truth.'

He got up and throwing his table napkin on the table with a movement of exasperation, he turned round and flung his chair against the wall, and then went out without another word, while she, uttering a deep sigh, as if after a first victory, went on in a calm voice: 'You must not pay any attention to what your father has just said, my darlings; he was very much upset a short time ago, but he will be all right again in a few days.'

Then she talked with the abbe and Miss Smith and had tender, pretty words for all her children, those sweet, tender mother's ways which unfold little hearts.

When dinner was over she went into the drawing-room, all her children following her. She made the elder ones chatter, and when their bedtime came she kissed them for a long time and then went alone into her room.

She waited, for she had no doubt that the count would come, and she made up her mind then, as her children were not with her, to protect herself as a woman of the world as she would protect her life, and in the pocket of her dress she put the little loaded revolver which she had bought a few days previously. The hours went by, the hours struck, and every sound was hushed in the house. Only the cabs, continued to rumble through the streets, but their noise was only heard vaguely through the shuttered and curtained windows.

She waited, full of nervous energy, without any fear of him now, ready for anything, and almost triumphant, for she had found means of torturing him continually during every moment of his life.

But the first gleam of dawn came in through the fringe at the bottom of her curtain without his having come into her room, and then she awoke to the fact, with much amazement, that he was not coming. Having locked and bolted her door, for greater security, she went to bed at last and remained there, with her eyes open, thinking and barely understanding it all, without being able to guess what he was going to do.

When her maid brought her tea she at the same time handed her a letter from her husband. He told her that he was going to undertake a longish journey and in a postscript added that his lawyer would provide her with any sums of money she might require for all her expenses.

It was at the opera, between two acts of 'Robert the Devil.' In the stalls the men were standing up, with their hats on, their waistcoats cut very low so as to show a large amount of white shirt front, in which gold and jewelled studs glistened, and were looking at the boxes full of ladies in low dresses covered with diamonds and pearls, who were expanding like flowers in that illuminated hothouse, where the beauty of their faces and the whiteness of their shoulders seemed to bloom in order to be gazed at, amid the sound of the music and of human voices.

Two friends, with their backs to the orchestra, were scanning those rows of elegance, that exhibition of real or false charms, of jewels, of luxury and of pretension which displayed itself in all parts of the Grand Theatre, and one of them, Roger de Salnis, said to his companion, Bernard Grandin:

'Just look how beautiful the Comtesse de Mascaret still is.'

The older man in turn looked through his opera glasses at a tall lady in a box opposite. She appeared to be still very young, and her striking beauty seemed to attract all eyes in every corner of the house. Her pale complexion, of an ivory tint, gave her the appearance of a statue, while a small diamond coronet glistened on her black hair like a streak of light.

When he had looked at her for some time, Bernard Grandin replied with a jocular accent of sincere conviction: 'You may well call her beautiful!'

'How old do you think she is?'

'Wait a moment. I can tell you exactly, for I have known her since she was a child and I saw her make her debut into society when she was quite a girl. She is—she is—thirty—thirty-six.'

'Impossible!'

'I am sure of it.'

'She looks twenty-five.'

'She has had seven children.'

'It is incredible.'

'And what is more, they are all seven alive, as she is a very good mother. I occasionally go to the house, which is a very quiet and pleasant one, where one may see the phenomenon of the family in the midst of society.'

'How very strange! And have there never been any reports about her?'

'Never.'

'But what about her husband? He is peculiar, is he not?'

'Yes and no. Very likely there has been a little drama between them, one of those little domestic dramas which one suspects, never finds out exactly, but guesses at pretty closely.'

'What is it?'

'I do not know anything about it. Mascaret leads a very fast life now, after being a model husband. As long as he remained a good spouse he had a shocking temper, was crabbed and easily took offence, but since he has been leading his present wild life he has become quite different, But one might surmise that he has some trouble, a worm gnawing somewhere, for he has aged very much.'

Thereupon, the two friends talked philosophically for some minutes about the secret, unknowable troubles which differences of character or perhaps physical antipathies, which were not perceived at first, give rise to in families, and then Roger de Salnis, who was still looking at Madame de Mascaret through his opera glasses, said: 'It is almost incredible that that woman can have had seven children!'

'Yes, in eleven years; after which, when she was thirty, she refused to have any more, in order to take her place in society, which she seems likely to do for many years.'

'Poor women!'

'Why do you pity them?'

'Why? Ah! My dear fellow, just consider! Eleven years in a condition of motherhood for such a woman! What a hell! All her youth, all her beauty, every hope of success, every poetical ideal of a brilliant life sacrificed to that abominable law of reproduction which turns the normal woman into a mere machine for bringing children into the world.'

'What would you have? It is only Nature!'

'Yes, but I say that Nature is our enemy, that we must always fight against Nature, for she is continually bringing us back to an animal state. You may be sure that God has not put anything on this earth that is clean, pretty, elegant or accessory to our ideal; the human brain has done it. It is man who has introduced a little grace, beauty, unknown charm and mystery into creation by singing about it, interpreting it, by admiring it as a poet, idealizing it as an artist and by explaining it through science, doubtless making mistakes, but finding ingenious reasons, hidden grace and beauty, unknown charm and mystery in the various phenomena of Nature. God created only coarse beings, full of the germs of disease, who, after a few years of bestial enjoyment, grow old and infirm, with all the ugliness and all the want of power of human decrepitude. He seems to have made them only in order that they may reproduce their species in an ignoble manner and then die like ephemeral insects. I said reproduce their species in an ignoble manner and I adhere to that expression. What is there as a matter of fact more ignoble and more repugnant than that act of reproduction of living beings, against which all delicate minds always have revolted and always will revolt? Since all the organs which have been invented by this economical and malicious Creator serve two purposes, why did He not choose another method of performing that sacred mission, which is the noblest and the most exalted of all human functions? The mouth, which nourishes the body by means of material food, also diffuses abroad speech and thought. Our flesh renews itself of its own accord, while we are thinking about it. The olfactory organs, through which the vital air reaches the lungs, communicate all the perfumes of the world to the brain: the smell of flowers, of woods, of trees, of the sea. The ear, which enables us to communicate with our fellow men, has also allowed us to invent music, to create dreams, happiness, infinite and even physical pleasure by means of sound! But one might say that the cynical and cunning Creator wished to prohibit man from ever ennobling and idealizing his intercourse with women. Nevertheless man has found love, which is not a bad reply to that sly Deity, and he has adorned it with so much poetry that woman often forgets the sensual part of it. Those among us who are unable to deceive themselves have invented vice and refined debauchery, which is another way of laughing at God and paying homage, immodest homage, to beauty.

'But the normal man begets children just like an animal

coupled with another by law.

'Look at that woman! Is it not abominable to think that such a jewel, such a pearl, born to be beautiful, admired, feted and adored, has spent eleven years of her life in providing heirs for the Comte de Mascaret?'

Bernard Grandin replied with a laugh: 'There is a great deal of truth in all that, but very few people would understand you.'

Salnis became more and more animated. 'Do you know how I picture God myself?' he said. 'As an enormous, creative organ beyond our ken, who scatters millions of worlds into space, just as one single fish would deposit its spawn in the sea. He creates because it is His function as God to do so, but He does not know what He is doing and is stupidly prolific in His work and is ignorant of the combinations of all kinds which are produced by His scattered germs. The human mind is a lucky little local, passing accident which was totally unforeseen, and condemned to disappear with this earth and to recommence perhaps here or elsewhere the same or different with fresh combinations of eternally new beginnings. We owe it to this little lapse of intelligence on His part that we are very uncomfortable in this world which was not made for us, which had not been prepared to receive us, to lodge and feed us or to satisfy reflecting beings, and we owe it to Him also that we have to struggle without ceasing against what are still called the designs of Providence, when we are really refined and civilized beings.'

Grandin, who was listening to him attentively as he had long known the surprising outbursts of his imagination, asked him: 'Then you believe that human thought is the spontaneous product of blind divine generation?'

'Naturally! A fortuitous function of the nerve centres of our brain, like the unforeseen chemical action due to new mixtures and similar also to a charge of electricity, caused by friction or the unexpected proximity of some substance, similar to all phenomena caused by the infinite and fruitful fermentation of living matter.

'But, my dear fellow, the truth of this must be evident to any one who looks about him. If the human mind, ordained by an omniscient Creator, had been intended to be what it has become, exacting, inquiring, agitated, tormented—so different from mere animal thought and resignation—would the world which was created to receive the beings which we now are have been this unpleasant little park for small game, this salad patch, this wooded, rocky and spherical kitchen garden where your improvident Providence had destined us to live naked, in caves or under trees, nourished on the flesh of slaughtered animals, our brethren, or on raw vegetables nourished by the sun and the rain?

'But it is sufficient to reflect for a moment, in order to understand that this world was not made for such creatures as we are. Thought, which is developed by a miracle in the nerves of the cells in our brain, powerless, ignorant and confused as it is, and as it will always remain, makes all of us who are intellectual beings eternal and wretched exiles on earth.

'Look at this earth, as God has given it to those who inhabit it. Is it not visibly and solely made, planted and covered with forests for the sake of animals? What is there for us? Nothing. And for them, everything, and they have nothing to do but to eat or go hunting and eat each other, according to their instincts, for God never foresaw gentleness and peaceable manners; He only foresaw the death of creatures which were bent on destroying and devouring each other. Are not the quail, the pigeon and the partridge the natural prey of the hawk? The sheep, the stag and the ox that of the great flesh-eating animals, rather than meat to be fattened and served up to us with truffles, which have been unearthed by pigs for our special benefit?

'As to ourselves, the more civilized, intellectual and refined we are, the more we ought to conquer and subdue that animal instinct, which represents the will of God in us. And so, in order to mitigate our lot as brutes, we have discovered and made everything, beginning with houses, then exquisite food, sauces, sweetmeats, pastry, drink, stuffs, clothes, ornaments, beds, mattresses, carriages, railways and innumerable machines, besides arts and sciences, writing and poetry. Every ideal comes from us as do all the amenities of life, in order to make our existence as simple reproducers, for which divine Providence solely intended us, less monotonous and less hard.

'Look at this theatre. Is there not here a human world created by us, unforeseen and unknown to eternal fate, intelligible to our minds alone, a sensual and intellectual distraction, which has been invented solely by and for that discontented and restless little animal, man?

'Look at that woman, Madame de Mascaret. God intended her to live in a cave, naked or wrapped up in the skins of wild animals. But is she not better as she is? But, speaking of her, does any one know why and how her brute of a husband, having such a companion by his side, and especially after having been boorish enough to make her a mother seven times, has suddenly left her, to run after bad women?'

Grandin replied: 'Oh! My dear fellow, this is probably the only reason. He found that raising a family was becoming too expensive, and from reasons of domestic economy he has arrived at the same principles which you lay down as a philosopher.'

Just then the curtain rose for the third act, and they turned round, took off their hats and sat down.

The Comte and Comtesse Mascaret were sitting side by side in the carriage which was taking them home from the Opera, without speaking but suddenly the husband said to his wife: 'Gabrielle!'

'What do you want?'

'Don't you think that this has lasted long enough?'

'What?'

'The horrible punishment to which you have condemned me for the last six years?'

'What do you want? I cannot help it.'

'Then tell me which of them it is.'

'Never.'

'Think that I can no longer see my children or feel them round me, without having my heart burdened with this doubt. Tell me which of them it is, and I swear that I will forgive you and treat it like the others.'

'I have not the right to do so.'

'Do you not see that I can no longer endure this life, this thought which is wearing me out, or this question which I am constantly asking myself, this question which tortures me each time I look at them? It is driving me mad.'

'Then you have suffered a great deal?' she said.

'Terribly. Should I, without that, have accepted the horror of living by your side, and the still greater horror of feeling and knowing that there is one among them whom I cannot recognize and who prevents me from loving the others?'

'Then you have really suffered very much?' she repeated.

And he replied in a constrained and sorrowful voice:

'Yes, for do I not tell you every day that it is intolerable torture to me? Should I have remained in that house, near you and them, if I did not love them? Oh! You have behaved abominably toward me. All the affection of my heart I have bestowed upon my children, and that you know. I am for them a father of the olden time, as I was for you a husband of one of the families of old, for by instinct I have remained a natural man, a man of former days. Yes, I will confess it, you have made me terribly jealous, because you are a woman of another race, of another soul, with other requirements. Oh! I shall never forget the things you said to me, but from that day I troubled myself no more about you. I did not kill you, because then I should have had no means on earth of ever discovering which of our—of your children is not mine. I have waited, but I have suffered more than you would believe, for I can no longer venture to love them, except, perhaps, the two eldest; I no longer venture to look at them, to call them to me, to kiss them; I cannot take them on my knee without asking myself, "Can it be this one?" I have been correct in my behavior toward you for six years, and even kind and complaisant. Tell me the truth, and I swear that I will do nothing unkind.'

He thought, in spite of the darkness of the carriage, that he could perceive that she was moved, and feeling certain that she was going to speak at last, he said: 'I beg you, I beseech you to tell me.'

'I have been more guilty than you think perhaps,' she replied, 'but I could no longer endure that life of continual motherhood, and I had only one means of driving you from me. I lied before God and I lied, with my hand raised to my children's head, for I never have wronged you.'

He seized her arm in the darkness, and squeezing it as he had done on that terrible day of their drive in the Bois de Boulogne, he stammered:

'Is that true?'

'It is true.'

But, wild with grief, he said with a groan: 'I shall have fresh doubts that will never end! When did you lie, the last time or now? How am I to believe you at present? How can one believe a woman after that? I shall never again know what I am to think. I would rather you had said to me, "It is Jacques or it is Jeanne."'

The carriage drove into the courtyard of the house and when it had drawn up in front of the steps the count alighted first, as usual, and offered his wife his arm to mount the stairs. As soon as they reached the first floor he said: 'May I speak to you for a few moments longer?' And she replied, 'I am quite willing.'

They went into a small drawing-room and a footman, in some surprise, lighted the wax candles. As soon as he had left the room and they were alone the count continued: 'How am I to know the truth? I have begged you a thousand times to speak, but you have remained dumb, impenetrable, inflexible, inexorable, and now today you tell me that you have been lying. For six years you have actually allowed me to believe such a thing! No, you are lying now, I do not know why, but out of pity for me, perhaps?'

She replied in a sincere and convincing manner: 'If I had not done so, I should have had four more children in the last six years!'

'Can a mother speak like that?'

'Oh!' she replied, 'I do not feel that I am the mother of children who never have been born; it is enough for me to be the mother of those that I have and to love them with all my heart. I am a woman of the civilized world, monsieur—we all are—and we are no longer, and we refuse to be, mere females to restock the earth.'

She got up, but he seized her hands. 'Only one word, Gabrielle. Tell me the truth!'

'I have just told you. I never have dishonored you.'

He looked her full in the face, and how beautiful she was, with her gray eyes, like the cold sky. In her dark hair sparkled the diamond coronet, like a radiance. He suddenly felt, felt by a kind of intuition, that this grand creature was not merely a being destined to perpetuate the race, but the strange and mysterious product of all our complicated desires which have been accumulating in us for centuries but which have been turned aside from their primitive and divine object and have wandered after a mystic, imperfectly perceived and intangible beauty. There are some women like that, who blossom only for our dreams, adorned with every poetical attribute of civilization, with that ideal luxury, coquetry and esthetic charm which surround woman, a living statue that brightens our life.

Her husband remained standing before her, stupefied at his tardy and obscure discovery, confusedly hitting on the cause of his former jealousy and understanding it all very imperfectly, and at last lie said: 'I believe you, for I feel at this moment that you are not lying, and before I really thought that you were.'

She put out her hand to him: 'We are friends then?'

He took her hand and kissed it and replied: 'We are friends. Thank you, Gabrielle.'

Then he went out, still looking at her, and surprised that she was still so beautiful and feeling a strange emotion arising in him.

17

THE BLIND MAN

How is it that the sunlight gives us such joy? Why does this radiance when it falls on the earth fill us with the joy of living? The whole sky is blue, the fields are green, the houses all white, and our enchanted eyes drink in those bright colors which bring delight to our souls. And then there springs up in our hearts, a desire to dance, to run, to sing, a happy lightness of thought, a sort of enlarged tenderness; we feel a longing to embrace the sun.

The blind, as they sit in the doorways, impassive in their eternal darkness, remain as calm as ever in the midst of this fresh gaiety, and, not understanding what is taking place around them, they continually check their dogs as they attempt to play.

When, at the close of the day, they are returning home on the arm of a young brother or a little sister, if the child says: 'It was a very fine day!' the other answers: 'I could notice that it was fine. Loulou wouldn't keep quiet.'

I knew one of these men whose life was one of the most cruel martyrdoms that could possibly be conceived.

He was a peasant, the son of a Norman farmer. As long as his father and mother lived, he was more or less taken care of; he suffered little save from his horrible infirmity; but as soon as the old people were gone, an atrocious life of misery commenced for him. Dependent on a sister of his, everybody in the farmhouse treated him as a beggar who is eating the bread of strangers. At every meal, the very food he swallowed was made a subject of reproach against him; he was called a drone, a clown, and although his brother-in-law had taken possession of his portion of the inheritance, he was helped grudgingly to soup, getting just enough to save him from starving.

His face was very pale and his two big white eyes looked like wafers. He remained unmoved at all the insults hurled at him, so reserved that one could not tell whether he felt them.

Moreover, he had never known any tenderness, his mother having always treated him unkindly and caring very little for him; for in country places useless persons are considered a nuisance, and the peasants would be glad to kill the infirm of their species, as poultry do.

As soon as he finished his soup, he went and sat outside the door in summer and in winter beside the fireside, and did not stir again all the evening. He made no gesture, no movement; only his eyelids, quivering from some nervous affection, fell down sometimes over his white, sightless orbs. Had he any intellect, any thinking faculty, any consciousness of his own existence? Nobody cared to inquire.

For some years things went on in this fashion. But his incapacity for work as well as his impassiveness eventually exasperated his relatives, and he became a laughingstock, a sort of butt for merriment, a prey to the inborn ferocity, to the savage gaiety of the brutes who surrounded him.

It is easy to imagine all the cruel practical jokes inspired by his blindness. And, in order to have some fun in return for feeding him, they now converted his meals into hours of pleasure for the neighbors and of punishment for the helpless creature himself.

The peasants from the nearest houses came to this entertainment; it was talked about from door to door, and every day the kitchen of the farmhouse was full of people. Sometimes, they placed before his plate, when he was beginning to eat his soup, some cat or dog. The animal instinctively perceived the man's infirmity, and, softly approaching, commenced eating noiselessly, lapping up the soup daintily; and, when they lapped the food rather noisily, rousing the poor fellow's attention, they would prudently scamper away to avoid the blow of the spoon directed at random by the blind man!

Then the spectators ranged along the wall would burst out laughing, nudge each other and stamp their feet on the floor. And he, without ever uttering a word, would continue eating with his right hand, while stretching out his left to protect his plate.

Another time, they made him chew corks, bits of wood, leaves or even filth, which he was unable to distinguish.

After this they got tired even of these practical jokes, and the brother-in-law, angry at having to support him always, struck him, cuffed him incessantly, laughing at his futile efforts to ward off or return the blows. Then came a new pleasure—the pleasure of smacking his face. And the plough-men, the servant girls and even every passing vagabond were every moment giving him cuffs, which caused his eyelashes to twitch spasmodically. He did not know where to hide himself and remained with his arms always held out to guard against people coming too close to him.

At last, he was forced to beg.

He was placed somewhere on the high-road on market-days, and as soon as he heard the sound of footsteps or the rolling of a vehicle, he reached out his hat, stammering:

'Charity, if you please!'

But the peasant is not lavish, and for whole weeks he did not bring back a sou.

Then he became the victim of furious, pitiless hatred. And this is how he died.

One winter the ground was covered with snow, and it was freezing hard. His brother-in-law led him one morning a great distance along the high road in order that he might solicit alms. The blind man was left there all day; and when night came on, the brother-in-law told the people of his house that he could find no trace of the mendicant. Then he added:

'Pooh! Best not bother about him! He was cold and got someone to take him away. Never fear! He's not lost. He'll turn up soon enough tomorrow to eat the soup.'

Next day, he did not come back.

After long hours of waiting, stiffened with the cold, feeling that he was dying, the blind man began to walk. Being unable to find his way along the road, owing to its thick coating of ice, he went on at random, falling into ditches, getting up again, without uttering a sound, his sole object being to find some house where he could take shelter.

But, by degrees, the descending snow made a numbness steal over him, and his feeble limbs being incapable of carrying him farther, he sat down in the middle of an open field. He did not get up again.

The white flakes which fell continuously buried him, so that his body, quite stiff and stark, disappeared under the incessant accumulation of their rapidly thickening mass, and nothing was left to indicate the place where he lay.

His relatives made a pretence of inquiring about him and searching for him for about a week. They even made a show of weeping.

The winter was severe, and the thaw did not set in quickly. Now, one Sunday, on their way to mass, the farmers noticed a great flight of crows, who were whirling incessantly above the open field, and then descending like a shower of black rain at the same spot, ever going and coming.

The following week, these gloomy birds were still there. There was a crowd of them up in the air, as if they had gathered from all corners of the horizon, and they swooped down with a great cawing into the shining snow, which they covered like black patches, and in which they kept pecking obstinately. A young fellow went to see what they were doing and discovered the body of the blind man, already half devoured, mangled. His wan eyes had disappeared, pecked out by the long, voracious beaks.

And I can never feel the glad radiance of sunlit days without sadly remembering and pondering over the fate of the beggar who was such an outcast in life that his horrible death was a relief to all who had known him.

18

THE DONKEY

There was not a breath of air stirring; a heavy mist was lying over the river. It was like a layer of cotton placed on the water. The banks themselves were indistinct, hidden behind strange fogs. But day was breaking and the hill was becoming visible. In the dawning light of day, the plaster houses began to appear like white spots. Cocks were crowing in the barnyard.

On the other side of the river, hidden behind the fogs, just opposite Frette, a slight noise from time to time broke the dead silence of the quiet morning. At times, it was an indistinct plashing, like the cautious advance of a boat, then again a sharp noise like the rattle of an oar and then the sound of something dropping in the water. Then silence.

Sometimes whispered words, coming perhaps from a distance, perhaps from quite near, pierced through these opaque mists. They passed by like wild birds which have slept in the rushes and which fly away at the first light of day, crossing the mist and uttering a low and timid sound which wakes their brothers along the shores.

Suddenly along the bank, near the village, a barely perceptible shadow appeared on the water. Then it grew, became more distinct and, coming out of the foggy curtain which hung over the river, a flatboat, manned by two men, pushed up on the grass.

The one who was rowing rose and took a pailful of fish from

the bottom of the boat, then he threw the dripping net over his shoulder. His companion, who had not made a motion, exclaimed: 'Say, Mailloche, get your gun and see if we can't land some rabbit along the shore.'

The other one answered: 'All right. I'll be with you in a minute.' Then he disappeared, in order to hide their catch.

The man who had stayed in the boat slowly filled his pipe and lighted it. His name was Labouise, but he was called Chicot, and was in partnership with Maillochon, commonly called Mailloche, to practice the doubtful and undefined profession of junk-gatherers along the shore.

They were a low order of sailors and they navigated regularly only in the months of famine. The rest of the time they acted as junk-gatherers. Rowing about on the river day and night, watching for any prey, dead or alive, poachers on the water and nocturnal hunters, sometimes ambushing venison in the Saint-Germain forests, sometimes looking for drowned people and searching their clothes, picking up floating rags and empty bottles; thus did Labouise and Maillochon live easily.

At times, they would set out on foot about noon and stroll along straight ahead. They would dine in some inn on the shore and leave again side by side. They would remain away for a couple of days; then one morning they would be seen rowing about in the tub which they called their boat.

At Joinville or at Nogent some boatman would be looking for his boat, which had disappeared one night, probably stolen, while twenty or thirty miles from there, on the Oise, some shopkeeper would be rubbing his hands, congratulating himself on the bargain he had made when he bought a boat the day before for fifty francs, which two men offered him as they were passing.

Maillochon reappeared with his gun wrapped up in rags. He was a man of forty or fifty, tall and thin, with the restless eye of people who are worried by legitimate troubles and of hunted animals. His open shirt showed his hairy chest, but he seemed never to have had any more hair on his face than a short brush of a mustache and a few stiff hairs under his lower lip. He was bald around the temples. When he took off the dirty cap that he wore his scalp seemed to be covered with a fluffy down, like the body of a plucked chicken.

Chicot, on the contrary, was red, fat, short and hairy. He looked like a raw beefsteak. He continually kept his left eye closed, as if he were aiming at something or at somebody, and when people jokingly cried to him, 'Open your eye, Labouise!' he would answer quietly: 'Never fear, sister, I open it when there's cause to.'

He had a habit of calling every one 'sister,' even his scavenger companion.

He took up the oars again, and once more the boat disappeared in the heavy mist, which was now turned snowy white in the pink-tinted sky.

'What kind of lead did you take, Maillochon?' Labouise asked.

'Very small, number nine; that's the best for rabbits.'

They were approaching the other shore so slowly, so quietly that no noise betrayed them. This bank belongs to the Saint-Germain forest and is the boundary line for rabbit hunting. It is covered with burrows hidden under the roots of trees, and the creatures at daybreak frisk about, running in and out of the holes.

Maillochon was kneeling in the bow, watching, his gun hidden on the floor. Suddenly he seized it, aimed, and the report echoed for some time throughout the quiet country.

Labouise, in a few strokes, touched the beach, and his companion, jumping to the ground, picked up a little gray rabbit, not yet dead.

Then the boat once more disappeared into the fog in order to get to the other side, where it could keep away from the game wardens.

The two men seemed to be riding easily on the water. The

weapon had disappeared under the board which served as a hiding place and the rabbit was stuffed into Chicot's loose shirt.

After about a quarter of an hour, Labouise asked: 'Well, sister, shall we get one more?'

'It will suit me,' Maillochon answered.

The boat started swiftly down the current. The mist, which was hiding both shores, was beginning to rise. The trees could be barely perceived, as through a veil, and the little clouds of fog were floating up from the water. When they drew near the island, the end of which is opposite Herblay, the two men slackened their pace and began to watch. Soon a second rabbit was killed.

Then they went down until they were half way to Conflans. Here they stopped their boat, tied it to a tree and went to sleep in the bottom of it.

From time to time Labouise would sit up and look over the horizon with his open eye. The last of the morning mist had disappeared and the large summer sun was climbing in the blue sky.

On the other side of the river the vineyard-covered hill stretched out in a semicircle. One house stood out alone at the summit. Everything was silent.

Something was moving slowly along the tow-path, advancing with difficulty. It was a woman dragging a donkey. The stubborn, stiff-jointed beast occasionally stretched out a leg in answer to its companion's efforts, and it proceeded thus, with outstretched neck and ears lying flat, so slowly that one could not tell when it would ever be out of sight.

The woman, bent double, was pulling, turning round occasionally to strike the donkey with a stick.

As soon as he saw her, Labouise exclaimed: 'Say, Mailloche!'

Mailloche answered: 'What's the matter?'

'Want to have some fun?'

'Of course!'

'Then hurry, sister; we're going to have a laugh.'

Chicot took the oars. When he had crossed the river he stopped opposite the woman and called:

'Hey, sister!'

The woman stopped dragging her donkey and looked.

Labouise continued: 'What are you doing—going to the locomotive show?'

The woman made no reply. Chicot continued:

'Say, your trotter's prime for a race. Where are you taking him at that speed?'

At last the woman answered: 'I'm going to Macquart, at Champioux, to have him killed. He's worthless.'

Labouise answered: 'You're right. How much do you think Macquart will give you for him?'

The woman wiped her forehead on the back of her hand and hesitated, saying: 'How do I know? Perhaps three francs, perhaps four.'

Chicot exclaimed: 'I'll give you five francs and your errand's done! How's that?'

The woman considered the matter for a second and then exclaimed: 'Done!'

The two men landed. Labouise grasped the animal by the bridle. Maillochon asked in surprise:

'What do you expect to do with that carcass?'

Chicot this time opened his other eye in order to express his gaiety. His whole red face was grinning with joy. He chuckled: 'Don't worry, sister. I've got my idea.'

He gave five francs to the woman, who then sat down by the road to see what was going to happen. Then Labouise, in great humor, got the gun and held it out to Maillochon, saying: 'Each one in turn; we're going after big game, sister. Don't get so near or you'll kill it right away! You must make the pleasure last a little.'

He placed his companion about forty paces from the victim.

The ass, feeling itself free, was trying to get a little of the tall grass, but it was so exhausted that it swayed on its legs as if it were about to fall.

Maillochon aimed slowly and said: 'A little pepper for the ears; watch, Chicot!' And he fired.

The tiny shot struck the donkey's long ears and he began to shake them in order to get rid of the stinging sensation. The two men were doubled up with laughter and stamped their feet with joy. The woman, indignant, rushed forward; she did not want her donkey to be tortured, and she offered to return the five francs. Labouise threatened her with a thrashing and pretended to roll up his sleeves. He had paid, hadn't he? Well, then, he would take a shot at her skirts, just to show that it didn't hurt. She went away, threatening to call the police. They could hear her protesting indignantly and cursing as she went her way.

Maillochon held out the gun to his comrade, saying: 'It's your turn, Chicot.'

Labouise aimed and fired. The donkey received the charge in his thighs, but the shot was so small and came from such a distance that he thought he was being stung by flies, for he began to thrash himself with his tail.

Labouise sat down to laugh more comfortably, while Maillochon reloaded the weapon, so happy that he seemed to sneeze into the barrel. He stepped forward a few paces, and, aiming at the same place that his friend had shot at, he fired again. This time the beast started, tried to kick and turned its head. At last, a little blood was running. It had been wounded and felt a sharp pain, for it tried to run away with a slow, limping, jerky gallop.

Both men darted after the beast, Maillochon with a long stride, Labouise with the short, breathless trot of a little man. But the donkey, tired out, had stopped, and, with a bewildered look, was watching his two murderers approach. Suddenly, he stretched his neck and began to bray.

Labouise, out of breath, had taken the gun. This time he walked right up close, as he did not wish to begin the chase over again.

When the poor beast had finished its mournful cry, like a last call for help, the man called: 'Hey, Mailloche! Come here, sister; I'm going to give him some medicine.' And while the other man was forcing the animal's mouth open, Chicot stuck the barrel of his gun down its throat, as if he were trying to make it drink a potion. Then he said: 'Look out, sister, here she goes!'

He pressed the trigger. The donkey stumbled back a few steps, fell down, tried to get up again and finally lay on its side and closed its eyes. The whole body was trembling, its legs were kicking as if it were, trying to run. A stream of blood was oozing through its teeth. Soon it stopped moving. It was dead.

The two men went along, laughing. It was over too quickly; they had not had their money's worth. Maillochon asked: 'Well, what are we going to do now?'

Labouise answered: 'Don't worry, sister. Get the thing on the boat; we're going to have some fun when night comes.'

They went and got the boat. The animal's body was placed on the bottom, covered with fresh grass, and the two men stretched out on it and went to sleep.

Toward noon, Labouise drew a bottle of wine, some bread and butter and raw onions from a hiding place in their muddy, worm-eaten boat, and they began to eat.

When the meal was over, they once more stretched out on the dead donkey and slept. At nightfall, Labouise awoke and shook his comrade, who was snoring like a buzzsaw. 'Come on, sister,' he ordered.

Maillochon began to row. As they had plenty of time, they went up the Seine slowly. They coasted along the reaches covered with water-lilies, and the heavy, mud-covered boat slipped over the lily pads and bent the flowers, which stood up again as soon as they had passed.

When they reached the wall of the Eperon, which separates the Saint-Germain forest from the Maisons-Laffitte Park, Labouise stopped his companion and explained his idea to him. Maillochon was moved by a prolonged, silent laugh.

They threw into the water the grass which had covered the body, took the animal by the feet and hid it behind some bushes. Then they got into their boat again and went to Maisons-Laffitte.

The night was perfectly black when they reached the wine shop of old man Jules. As soon as the dealer saw them he came up, shook hands with them and sat down at their table. They began to talk of one thing and another. By eleven o'clock, the last customer had left and old man Jules winked at Labouise and asked: 'Well, have you got any?'

Labouise made a motion with his head and answered: 'Perhaps so, perhaps not!'

The dealer insisted: 'Perhaps you've got nothing but gray ones?'

Chicot dug his hands into his flannel shirt, drew out the ears of a rabbit and declared: 'Three francs a pair!'

Then began a long discussion about the price. Two francs sixty-five and the two rabbits were delivered. As the two men were getting up to go, old man Jules, who had been watching them, exclaimed:

'You have something else, but you won't say what.'

Labouise answered. 'Possibly, but it is not for you; you're too stingy.'

The man, growing eager, kept asking: 'What is it? Something big? Perhaps we might make a deal.'

Labouise, who seemed perplexed, pretended to consult Maillochon with a glance. Then he answered in a slow voice: 'This is how it is. We were in the bushes at Eperon when something passed right near us, to the left, at the end of the wall. Mailloche takes a shot and it drops. We skipped on account of the game people. I can't tell you what it is, because I don't know. But it's big enough. But what is it? If I told you I'd be lying, and you know, sister, between us everything's above-board.'

Anxiously the man asked: 'Think it's venison?'

Labouise answered: 'Might be and then again it might not! Venison?—uh! uh!—might be a little big for that! Mind you, I don't say it's a doe, because I don't know, but it might be.'

Still the dealer insisted: 'Perhaps it's a buck?'

Labouise stretched out his hand, exclaiming: 'No, it's not that! It's not a buck. I should have seen the horns. No, it's not a buck!'

'Why didn't you bring it with you?' asked the man.

'Because, sister, from now on I sell from where I stand. Plenty of people will buy. All you have to do is to take a walk over there, find the thing and take it. No risk for me.'

The innkeeper, growing suspicious, exclaimed 'Supposing he wasn't there!'

Labouise once more raised his hand and said:

'He's there, I swear! First bush to the left. What it is, I don't know. But it's not a buck, I'm positive. It's for you to find out what it is. Twenty-five francs, cash down!'

Still the man hesitated: 'Couldn't you bring it?'

Maillochon exclaimed: 'No, indeed! You know our price! Take it or leave it!'

The dealer decided: 'It's a bargain for twenty francs!'

And they shook hands over the deal.

Then he took out four big five-franc pieces from the cash drawer, and the two friends pocketed the money. Labouise arose, emptied his glass and left. As he was disappearing in the shadows, he turned round to exclaim: 'It isn't a buck. I don't know what it is! But it's there. I'll give you back your money if you find nothing!'

And he disappeared in the darkness. Maillochon, who was following him, kept punching him in the back to express his joy.

19

THE PATRON

We never dreamed of such good fortune! The son of a provincial bailiff, Jean Marin had come, as do so many others, to study law in the Quartier Latin. In the various beerhouses that he had frequented, he had made friends with several talkative students who spouted politics as they drank their beer. He had a great admiration for them and followed them persistently from cafe to cafe, even paying for their drinks when he had the money.

He became a lawyer and pleaded causes, which he lost. However, one morning, he read in the papers that one of his former comrades of the Quartier had just been appointed deputy.

He again became his faithful hound, the friend who does the drudgery, the unpleasant tasks, for whom one sends when one has need of him and with whom one does not stand on ceremony. But it chanced through some parliamentary incident that the deputy became a minister. Six months later, Jean Marin was appointed a state councillor.

He was so elated with pride at first that he lost his head. He would walk through the streets just to show himself off, as though one could tell by his appearance what position he occupied. He managed to say to the shopkeepers as soon as he entered a store, bringing it in somehow in the course of the most insignificant remarks and even to the news vendors and the cabmen:

'I, who am a state councillor—'

Then, in consequence of his position as well as for professional reasons and as in duty bound through being an influential and generous man, he felt an imperious need of patronizing others. He offered his support to every one, on all occasions and with unbounded generosity.

When he met any one he recognized on the boulevards, he would advance to meet them with a charmed air, would take their hand, inquire after their health, and, without waiting for any questions, remark:

'You know I am state councillor, and I am entirely at your service. If I can be of any use to you, do not hesitate to call on me. In my position one has great influence.'

Then he would go into some cafe with the friend he had just met and ask for a pen and ink and a sheet of paper. 'Just one, waiter; it is to write a letter of recommendation.'

And he wrote ten, twenty, fifty letters of recommendation a day. He wrote them to the Cafe Americain, to Bignon's, to Tortoni's, to the Maison Doree, to the Cafe Riche, to the Helder, to the Cafe Anglais, to the Napolitain, everywhere, everywhere. He wrote them to all the officials of the republican government, from the magistrates to the ministers. And he was happy, perfectly happy.

One morning, as he was starting out to go to the council, it began to rain. He hesitated about taking a cab, but decided not to do so and set out on foot.

The rain came down in torrents, swamping the sidewalks and inundating the streets. M. Marin was obliged to take shelter in a doorway. An old priest was standing there—an old priest with white hair. Before he became a councillor, M. Marin did not like the clergy. Now he treated them with consideration, ever since a cardinal had consulted him on an important matter. The rain continued to pour down in floods and obliged the two men to take shelter in the porter's lodge so as to avoid getting wet. M. Marin, who was always itching to talk so as to let people know who he was, remarked:

'This is horrible weather, Monsieur l'Abbe.'

The old priest bowed:

'Yes indeed, sir, it is very unpleasant when one comes to Paris for only a few days.'

'Ah! You come from the provinces?'

'Yes, monsieur. I am only passing through on my journey.'

'It certainly is very disagreeable to have rain during the few days one spends in the capital. We officials who stay here the year round, we think nothing of it.'

The priest did not reply. He was looking at the street where the rain seemed to be falling less heavily. And with a sudden resolve he raised his cassock just as women raise their skirts in stepping across water.

M. Marin, seeing him start away, exclaimed:

'You will get drenched, Monsieur l'Abbe. Wait a few moments longer; the rain will be over.'

The good man stopped irresistibly and then said:

'But I am in a great hurry. I have an important engagement.'

M. Marin seemed quite worried.

'But you will be absolutely drenched. Might I ask in which direction you are going?'

The priest appeared to hesitate. Then he said:

'I am going in the direction of the Palais Royal.'

'In that case, if you will allow me, Monsieur l'Abbe, I will offer you the shelter of my umbrella. As for me, I am going to the council. I am a councillor of state.'

The old priest raised his head and looked at his neighbor and then exclaimed:

'I thank you, monsieur. I shall be glad to accept your offer.'

M. Marin then took his arm and led him away. He directed him, watched over him and advised him.

'Be careful of that stream, Monsieur l'Abbe. And be very careful about the carriage wheels; they spatter you with mud sometimes from head to foot. Look out for the umbrellas of the people passing by; there is nothing more dangerous to the eyes than the tips of the ribs. Women especially are unbearable; they pay no heed to where they are going and always jab you in the face with the point of their parasols or umbrellas. And they never move aside for anybody. One would suppose the town belonged to them. They monopolize the pavement and the street. It is my opinion that their education has been greatly neglected.'

And M. Marin laughed.

The priest did not reply. He walked along, slightly bent over, picking his steps carefully so as not to get mud on his boots or his cassock.

M. Marin resumed:

'I suppose you have come to Paris to divert your mind a little?'

The good man replied:

'No, I have some business to attend to.'

'Ah! Is it important business? Might I venture to ask what it is? If I can be of any service to you, you may command me.'

The priest seemed embarrassed. He murmured:

'Oh, it is a little personal matter; a little difficulty with—with my bishop. It would not interest you. It is a matter of internal regulation—an ecclesiastical affair.'

M. Marin was eager.

'But it is precisely the state council that regulates all those things. In that case, make use of me.'

'Yes, monsieur, it is to the council that I am going. You are a thousand times too kind. I have to see M. Lerepere and M. Savon and also perhaps M. Petitpas.'

M. Marin stopped short.

'Why, those are my friends, Monsieur l'Abbe, my best friends, excellent colleagues, charming men. I will speak to them about you, and very highly. Count upon me.'

The cure thanked him, apologizing for troubling him, and stammered out a thousand grateful promises.

M. Marin was enchanted.

'Ah, you may be proud of having made a stroke of luck, Monsieur l'Abbe. You will see—you will see that, thanks to me, your affair will go along swimmingly.'

They reached the council hall. M. Marin took the priest into his office, offered him a chair in front of the fire and sat down himself at his desk and began to write.

'My dear colleague, allow me to recommend to you most highly a venerable and particularly worthy and deserving priest, M. L'Abbe—'

He stopped and asked:

'Your name, if you please?'

'L'Abbe Ceinture.'

'M. l'Abbe Ceinture, who needs your good office in a little matter which he will communicate to you.

'I am pleased at this incident which gives me an opportunity, my dear colleague—'

And he finished with the usual compliments.

When he had written the three letters he handed them to his protege, who took his departure with many protestations of gratitude.

M. Marin attended to some business and then went home, passed the day quietly, slept well, woke in a good humor and sent for his newspapers.

The first he opened was a radical sheet. He read:

'OUR CLERGY AND OUR GOVERNMENT OFFICIALS

'We shall never make an end of enumerating the misdeeds of the clergy. A certain priest, named Ceinture, convicted of conspiracy against the present government, accused of base actions to which we will not even allude, suspected besides of being a former Jesuit, metamorphosed into a simple priest, suspended by a bishop for causes that are said to be unmentionable and summoned to Paris to give an explanation of his conduct, has found an ardent defender in the man named Marin, a councillor of state, who was not afraid to give this frocked malefactor the warmest letters of recommendation to all the republican officials, his colleagues.

'We call the attention of the ministry to the unheard of attitude of this councillor of state—'

M. Marin bounded out of bed, dressed himself and hastened to his colleague, Petitpas, who said to him:

'How now? You were crazy to recommend to me that old conspirator!'

M. Marin, bewildered, stammered out:

'Why no—you see—I was deceived. He looked such an honest man. He played me a trick—a disgraceful trick! I beg that you will sentence him severely, very severely. I am going to write. Tell me to whom I should write about having him punished. I will go and see the attorney-general and the archbishop of Paris—yes, the archbishop.'

And seating himself abruptly at M. Petitpas' desk, he wrote:

'Monseigneur, I have the honor to bring to your grace's notice the fact that I have recently been made a victim of the intrigues and lies of a certain Abbe Ceinture, who imposed on my kind-heartedness.

'Deceived by the representations of this ecclesiastic, I was led—'

Then, having signed and sealed his letter, he turned to his colleague and exclaimed:

'See here, my dear friend, let this be a warning to you never to recommend any one again.'

20

THE DOOR

'Bah!' exclaimed Karl Massouligny, 'the question of complaisant husbands is a difficult one. I have seen many kinds, and yet I am unable to give an opinion about any of them. I have often tried to determine whether they are blind, weak or clairvoyant. I believe that there are some which belong to each of these categories.

'Let us quickly pass over the blind ones. They cannot rightly be called complaisant, since they do not know, but they are good creatures who cannot see farther than their nose. It is a curious and interesting thing to notice the ease with which men and women can be deceived. We are taken in by the slightest trick of those who surround us, by our children, our friends, our servants, our tradespeople. Humanity is credulous, and in order to discover deceit in others, we do not display one-tenth the shrewdness which we use when we, in turn, wish to deceive some one else.

'Clairvoyant husbands may be divided into three classes: Those who have some interest, pecuniary, ambitious or otherwise, in their wife's having love affairs. These ask only to safeguard appearances as much as possible, and they are satisfied.

'Next come those who get angry. What a beautiful novel one could write about them!

'Finally the weak ones! Those who are afraid of scandal.

'There are also those who are powerless, or, rather, tired,

who flee from the duties of matrimony through fear of ataxia or apoplexy, who are satisfied to see a friend run these risks.

'But I once met a husband of a rare species, who guarded against the common accident in a strange and witty manner.

'In Paris, I had made the acquaintance of an elegant, fashionable couple. The woman, nervous, tall, slender, courted, was supposed to have had many love adventures. She pleased me with her wit, and I believe that I pleased her also. I courted her, a trial courting to which she answered with evident provocations. Soon we got to tender glances, hand pressures, all the little gallantries which precede the final attack.

'Nevertheless, I hesitated. I consider that, as a rule, the majority of society intrigues, however short they may be, are not worth the trouble which they give us and the difficulties which may arise. I therefore mentally compared the advantages and disadvantages which I might expect, and I thought I noticed that the husband suspected me.

'One evening, at a ball, as I was saying tender things to the young woman in a little parlour leading from the big hall where the dancing was going on, I noticed in a mirror the reflection of some one who was watching me. It was he. Our looks met and then I saw him turn his head and walk away.

'I murmured: "Your husband is spying on us."

'She seemed dumbfounded and asked: "My husband?"

"Yes, he has been watching us for some time:

"Nonsense! Are you sure?"

"Very sure."

"How strange! He is usually extraordinarily pleasant to all my friends."

"Perhaps he guessed that I love you!"

"Nonsense! You are not the first one to pay attention to me. Every woman who is a little in view drags behind her a herd of admirers."

"Yes. But I love you deeply."

"Admitting that that is true, does a husband ever guess those things?"

"Then he is not jealous?"

"No-no!"

'She thought for an instant and then continued: "'No. I do not think that I ever noticed any jealousy on his part."'

"Has he never watched you?"

"No. As I said, he is always agreeable to my friends."

'From that day my courting became much more assiduous. The woman did not please me any more than before, but the probable jealousy of her husband tempted me greatly.

'As for her, I judged her coolly and clearly. She had a certain worldly charm, due to a quick, gay, amiable and superficial mind, but no real, deep attraction. She was, as I have already said, an excitable little being, all on the surface, with rather a showy elegance. How can I explain myself? She was an ornament, not a home.

'One day, after taking dinner with her, her husband said to me, just as I was leaving: "My dear friend" (he now called me "friend"), "we soon leave for the country. It is a great pleasure to my wife and myself to entertain people whom we like. We would be very pleased to have you spend a month with us. It would be very nice of you to do so."

'I was dumbfounded, but I accepted.

'A month later I arrived at their estate of Vertcresson, in Touraine. They were waiting for me at the station, five miles from the chateau. There were three of them, she, the husband and a gentleman unknown to me, the Comte de Morterade, to whom I was introduced. He appeared to be delighted to make my acquaintance, and the strangest ideas passed through my mind while we trotted along the beautiful road between two hedges. I was saying to myself: "Let's see, what can this mean? Here is a husband who cannot doubt that his wife and I are on more than friendly terms, and yet he invites me to his house, receives me like an old friend and seems to say: "Go ahead, my friend, the road is clear!"

'Then I am introduced to a very pleasant gentleman, who seems already to have settled down in the house, and—and who is perhaps trying to get out of it, and who seems as pleased at my arrival as the husband himself.

'Is it some former admirer who wishes to retire? One might think so. But, then, would these two men tacitly have come to one of these infamous little agreements so common in society? And it is proposed to me that I should quietly enter into the pact and carry it out. All hands and arms are held out to me. All doors and hearts are open to me.

'And what about her? An enigma. She cannot be ignorant of everything. However—however—well, I cannot understand it.

'The dinner was very gay and cordial. On leaving the table, the husband and his friend began to play cards, while I went out on the porch to look at the moonlight with madame. She seemed to be greatly affected by nature, and I judged that the moment for my happiness was near. That evening she was really delightful. The country had seemed to make her more tender. Her long, slender waist looked pretty on this stone porch beside a great vase in which grew some flowers. I felt like dragging her out under the trees, throwing myself at her feet and speaking to her words of love.

'Her husband's voice called "Louise!"

"Yes, dear."

"You are forgetting the tea."

"I'll go and see about it, my friend."

'We returned to the house, and she gave us some tea. When the two men had finished playing cards, they were visibly tired. I had to go to my room. I did not get to sleep till late, and then I slept badly.

'An excursion was decided upon for the following afternoon, and we went in an open carriage to visit some ruins. She and I were in the back of the vehicle and they were opposite us, riding backward. The conversation was sympathetic and agreeable. I am an orphan, and it seemed to me as though I had just found my family, I felt so at home with them.

'Suddenly, as she had stretched out her foot between her husband's legs, he murmured reproachfully: "Louise, please don't wear out your old shoes yourself. There is no reason for being neater in Paris than in the country."

'I lowered my eyes. She was indeed wearing worn-out shoes, and I noticed that her stockings were not pulled up tight.

'She had blushed and hidden her foot under her dress. The friend was looking out in the distance with an indifferent and unconcerned look.

'The husband offered me a cigar, which I accepted. For a few days, it was impossible for me to be alone with her for two minutes; he was with us everywhere. He was delightful to me, however.

'One morning, he came to get me to take a walk before breakfast, and the conversation happened to turn on marriage. I spoke a little about solitude and about how charming life can be made by the affection of a woman. Suddenly, he interrupted me, saying: "My friend, don't talk about things you know nothing about. A woman who has no other reason for loving you will not love you long. All the little coquetries which make them so exquisite when they do not definitely belong to us cease as soon as they become ours. And then—the respectable women—that is to say our wives—are—are not—in fact do not understand their profession of wife. Do you understand?"

'He said no more, and I could not guess his thoughts.

'Two days after this conversation he called me to his room quite early, in order to show me a collection of engravings. I sat in an easy chair opposite the big door which separated his apartment from his wife's, and behind this door I heard some one walking and moving, and I was thinking very little of the engravings, although I kept exclaiming: "Oh, charming! Delightful! Exquisite!"

'He suddenly said: "Oh, I have a beautiful specimen in the next room. I'll go and get it."

'He ran to the door quickly, and both sides opened as though for a theatrical effect.

'In a large room, all in disorder, in the midst of skirts, collars, waists lying around on the floor, stood a tall, dried-up creature. The lower part of her body was covered with an old, worn-out silk petticoat, which was hanging limply on her shapeless form, and she was standing in front of a mirror brushing some short, sparse blond hairs. Her arms formed two acute angles, and as she turned around in astonishment, I saw under a common cotton chemise a regular cemetery of ribs, which were hidden from the public gaze by well-arranged pads.

'The husband uttered a natural exclamation and came back, closing the doors, and said: "Gracious! how stupid I am! Oh, how thoughtless! My wife will never forgive me for that!"

'I already felt like thanking him. I left three days later, after cordially shaking hands with the two men and kissing the lady's fingers. She bade me a cold good-bye.'

Karl Massouligny was silent. Some one asked: 'But what was the friend?'

'I don't know—however—however he looked greatly distressed to see me leaving so soon.'

21

A SALE

The defendants, Cesaire-Isidore Brument and Prosper-Napoleon Cornu, appeared before the Court of Assizes of the Seine-Inferieure, on a charge of attempted murder, by drowning, of Mme. Brument, lawful wife of the first of the aforenamed.

The two prisoners sat side by side on the traditional bench. They were two peasants; the first was small and stout, with short arms, short legs, and a round head with a red pimply face, planted directly on his trunk, which was also round and short, and with apparently no neck. He was a raiser of pigs and lived at Cacheville-la-Goupil, in the district of Criquetot.

Cornu (Prosper-Napoleon) was thin, of medium height, with enormously long arms. His head was on crooked, his jaw awry, and he squinted. A blue blouse, as long as a shirt, hung down to his knees, and his yellow hair, which was scanty and plastered down on his head, gave his face a worn-out, dirty look, a dilapidated look that was frightful. He had been nicknamed 'the cure' because he could imitate to perfection the chanting in church, and even the sound of the serpent. This talent attracted to his cafe—for he was a saloon keeper at Criquetot—a great many customers who preferred the 'mass at Cornu' to the mass in church.

Mme. Brument, seated on the witness bench, was a thin peasant woman who seemed to be always asleep. She sat there motionless, her hands crossed on her knees, gazing fixedly before her with a stupid expression.

The judge continued his interrogation.

'Well, then, Mme. Brument, they came into your house and threw you into a barrel full of water. Tell us the details. Stand up.'

She rose. She looked as tall as a flag pole with her cap which looked like a white skull cap. She said in a drawling tone:

'I was shelling beans. Just then they came in. I said to myself, 'What is the matter with them? They do not seem natural, they seem up to some mischief." They watched me sideways, like this, especially Cornu, because he squints. I do not like to see them together, for they are two good-for-nothings when they are in company. I said: "What do you want with me?" They did not answer. I had a sort of mistrust—'

The defendant Brument interrupted the witness hastily, saying: 'I was full.'

Then Cornu, turning towards his accomplice said in the deep tones of an organ:

'Say that we were both full, and you will be telling no lie.'

The judge, severely:

'You mean by that that you were both drunk?'

Brument: 'There can be no question about it.'

Cornu: 'That might happen to anyone.'

The judge to the victim: 'Continue your testimony, woman Brument.'

'Well, Brument said to me, "Do you wish to earn a hundred sous?" "Yes," I replied, seeing that a hundred sous are not picked up in a horse's tracks. Then he said: "Open your eyes and do as I do," and he went to fetch the large empty barrel which is under the rain pipe in the corner, and he turned it over and brought it into my kitchen, and stuck it down in the middle of the floor, and then he said to me: "Go and fetch water until it is full."

'So I went to the pond with two pails and carried water, and still more water for an hour, seeing that the barrel was as large as a vat, saving your presence, m'sieu le president.

'All this time Brument and Cornu were drinking a glass, and then another glass, and then another. They were finishing their drinks when I said to them: "You are full, fuller than this barrel." And Brument answered me. "Do not worry, go on with your work, your turn will come, each one has his share." I paid no attention to what he said as he was full.

'When the barrel was full to the brim, I said: "There, that's done."

'And then Cornu gave me a hundred sous, not Brument, Cornu; it was Cornu gave them to me. And Brument said: "Do you wish to earn a hundred sous more?" "Yes," I said, for I am not accustomed to presents like that. Then he said: "Take off your clothes!"

"Take off my clothes?"

"Yes," he said.

"How many shall I take off?"

"If it worries you at all, keep on your chemise, that won't bother us."

'A hundred sous is a hundred sous, and I have to undress myself; but I did not fancy undressing before those two good-for-nothings. I took off my cap, and then my jacket, and then my skirt, and then my sabots. Brument said, "Keep on your stockings, also; we are good fellows."

'And Cornu said, too, "We are good fellows."

'So there I was, almost like mother Eve. And they got up from their chairs, but could not stand straight, they were so full, saving your presence, M'sieu le president.

'I said to myself: "What are they up to?"

'And Brument said: "Are you ready?"

'And Cornu said: "I'm ready!"

'And then they took me, Brument by the head, and Cornu

by the feet, as one might take, for instance, a sheet that has been washed. Then I began to bawl.

'And Brument said: "Keep still, wretched creature!"

'And they lifted me up in the air and put me into the barrel, which was full of water, so that I had a check of the circulation, a chill to my very insides.

'And Brument said: "Is that all?"

'Cornu said: "That is all."

'Brument said: "The head is not in, that will make a difference in the measure."

'Cornu said: "Put in her head."

'And then Brument pushed down my head as if to drown me, so that the water ran into my nose, so that I could already see Paradise. And he pushed it down, and I disappeared.

'And then he must have been frightened. He pulled me out and said: "Go and get dry, carcass."

'As for me, I took to my heels and ran as far as M. le cure's. He lent me a skirt belonging to his servant, for I was almost in a state of nature, and he went to fetch Maitre Chicot, the country watchman who went to Criquetot to fetch the police who came to my house with me.

'Then we found Brument and Cornu fighting each other like two rams.

'Brument was bawling: "It isn't true, I tell you that there is at least a cubic metre in it. It is the method that was no good."

'Cornu bawled: "Four pails, that is almost half a cubic metre. You need not reply, that's what it is."

'The police captain put them both under arrest. I have no more to tell.'

She sat down. The audience in the court room laughed. The jurors looked at one another in astonishment. The judge said:

'Defendant Cornu, you seem to have been the instigator of this infamous plot. What have you to say?'

And Cornu rose in his turn.

'Judge,' he replied, 'I was full.'

The Judge answered gravely:

'I know it. Proceed.'

'I will. Well, Brument came to my place about nine o'clock, and ordered two drinks, and said: "There's one for you, Cornu." I sat down opposite him and drank, and out of politeness, I offered him a glass. Then he returned the compliment and so did I, and so it went on from glass to glass until noon, when we were full.

'Then Brument began to cry. That touched me. I asked him what was the matter. He said: "I must have a thousand francs by Thursday." That cooled me off a little, you understand. Then he said to me all at once: "I will sell you my wife."

'I was full, and I was a widower. You understand, that stirred me up. I did not know his wife, but she was a woman, wasn't she? I asked him: "How much would you sell her for?"

'He reflected, or pretended to reflect. When one is full one is not very clear-headed, and he replied: "I will sell her by the cubic metre."

'That did not surprise me, for I was as drunk as he was, and I knew what a cubic metre is in my business. It is a thousand litres, that suited me.

'But the price remained to be settled. All depends on the quality. I said: "How much do you want a cubic metre?"

'He answered: "Two thousand francs."

'I gave a bound like a rabbit, and then I reflected that a woman ought not to measure more than three hundred litres. So I said: "That's too dear."

'He answered: 'I cannot do it for less. I should lose by it.'

'You understand, one is not a dealer in hogs for nothing. One understands one's business. But, if he is smart, the seller of bacon, I am smarter, seeing that I sell them also. Ha, Ha, Ha! So I said to him: "If she were new, I would not say anything, but she has been married to you for some time, so she is not as fresh as she was. I will give you fifteen hundred francs a cubic metre, not a sou more. Will that suit you?"

'He answered: "That will do. That's a bargain!"

'I agreed, and we started out, arm in arm. We must help each other in this world.

'But a fear came to me: "How can you measure her unless you put her into the liquid?"

'Then he explained his idea, not without difficulty for he was full. He said to me: "I take a barrel, and fill it with water to the brim. I put her in it. All the water that comes out we will measure, that is the way to fix it."

'I said: "I see, I understand. But this water that overflows will run away; how are you going to gather it up?"

'Then he began stuffing me and explained to me that all we should have to do would be to refill the barrel with the water his wife had displaced as soon as she should have left. All the water we should pour in would be the measure. I supposed about ten pails; that would be a cubic metre. He isn't a fool, all the same, when he is drunk, that old horse.

'To be brief, we reached his house and I took a look at its mistress. A beautiful woman she certainly was not. Anyone can see her, for there she is. I said to myself: "I am disappointed, but never mind, she will be of value; handsome or ugly, it is all the same, is it not, monsieur le president?" And then I saw that she was as thin as a rail. I said to myself: "She will not measure four hundred litres." I understand the matter, it being in liquids.

'She told you about the proceeding. I even let her keep on her chemise and stockings, to my own disadvantage.

'When that was done she ran away. I said: "Look out, Brument! she is escaping."

'He replied: "Do not be afraid. I will catch her all right. She will have to come back to sleep, I will measure the deficit."

'We measured. Not four pailfuls. Ha, Ha, Ha!'

The witness began to laugh so persistently that a gendarme was obliged to punch him in the back. Having quieted down, he resumed:

'In short, Brument exclaimed: "Nothing doing, that is not enough." I bawled and bawled, and bawled again, he punched me, I hit back. That would have kept on till the Day of judgment, seeing we were both drunk.

'Then came the gendarmes! They swore at us, they took us off to prison. I want damages.'

He sat down.

Brument confirmed in every particular the statements of his accomplice. The jury, in consternation, retired to deliberate.

At the end of an hour they returned a verdict of acquittal for the defendants, with some severe strictures on the dignity of marriage, and establishing the precise limitations of business transactions.

Brument went home to the domestic roof accompanied by his wife.

Cornu went back to his business.

ABOUT TERRY O'BRIEN

Terry O'Brien is an academic with three decades of experience in teaching language and communication skills in India and abroad. He also headed a college under the auspices of the University of Delhi.

A prolific writer, with several books to his credit, Terry O'Brien is a reputed professional motivational speaker and a quizmaster.

Made in the USA
Monee, IL
03 May 2026